ALSO BY MYRICK LAND

FICTION

Search the Dark Woods
Quicksand
Last Flight

NONFICTION

The Fine Art of Literary Mayhem
The Changing South (with Barbara Land)
Jungle Oil (with Barbara Land)
Lee: A Portrait of Lee Harvey Oswald by His Brother
(with Robert L. Oswald and Barbara Land)

THE DREAM BUYERS

THE DREAM BUYERS

♦ Myrick Land ♦

W · W · NORTON & COMPANY
NEW YORK   LONDON

Published simultaneously in Canada by George J. McLeod Limited,
Toronto. Printed in the United States of America.

First Edition

Library of Congress Cataloging in Publication Data

Land, Myrick, 1922–
   The dream buyers.

   I. Title.
PZ4.L25Dr 1980 [PS3562.A47]   813'.54   80–13967
ISBN 0–393–01393–6

1 2 3 4 5 6 7 8 9 0

For Barbara and Jackie,
Robert and Rosie

THE DREAM BUYERS

· 1 ·

Something Wrong
at Table Seven

"Brad?"

The telephone receiver vibrated with Charlie Diamond's deep voice.

"Yes, Mr. Diamond?" Donald Bradford said.

"How'd the vacation go?"

"Fine."

"The Bahamas, wasn't it?"

"Yes, that's right."

"Did you look in on the casino?"

"Yes, I did."

An expensive look, Bradford thought. Took every cent I had with me and eighteen thousand cabled to me reluctantly by Caleb Tompkins of the Reno National Bank, who has probably spent some sleepless nights since then, wondering why he let me talk him into it. Eighteen thousand—all gone in less than ninety minutes.

Examined coldly, away from the 21 tables, those ninety disastrous minutes were impossible to explain. Bradford could not recapture the delusion that led him on, the absolute certainty he had felt there in the Paradise Island Casino that through the cards that were about to fall all his problems would be solved, his life would be changed. After fifteen years of working around casinos in Reno, he had behaved like some wheat farmer from Kansas, betting money he did not have.

He felt guilty too about poor Tompkins, who'd allowed himself to be persuaded to cable the money against his better judgment.

"Was the place busy?" Diamond asked.

"Jammed. It's like going into a cave, entering the casino there after you've been out on the beaches, but every table was crowded."

Diamond was silent for a second, probably checking off a note on his desk calendar that reminded him to ask about Bradford's vacation. It would be one of twenty or thirty reminders listed there in his angular handwriting.

Bradford could picture him at his massive mahogany desk: neat, gray, carefully barbered, dressed in one of his quietly expensive gray suits. It was difficult now to detect any sign of that distant childhood when Charlie Diamond had traveled from one dusty western town to another with his father, helping him set up the ancient Century Wheel in hastily erected carnival tents, then waiting for the rubes to appear. Gambling was illegal in most of the towns visited by the sleazy carnivals Diamond's father accompanied, and there was always the danger that fundamentalist preachers would denounce the devilish Century Wheel and that Charlie and his father would have to escape in the middle of the night to avoid arrest by sheriffs goaded into action by the ministers.

Diamond had retained one souvenir from those days—the elaborately carved Century Wheel itself, enshrined for forty years on the main floor of the Diamond Mine, still attracting the rubes, still faithfully holding back thirty-one cents out of every dollar played on it.

"Something has come up that I'd like you to check on for me, Brad."

The polite chit-chat about his vacation was over. This was the voice of the monarch of the Diamond Mine, ready now to issue one of his soft commands. A deep voice, with one unexpected characteristic—an occasional hesitation, the remnant of a stammer which a few of the older employees remembered well from his early days in Reno. In a man who always seemed so completely self-assured, this one sign of fear remained, almost hidden but not entirely conquered after all these successful decades—a heritage perhaps from those years of wandering through sometimes hostile territory with his father, half expecting attack and enforced flight.

"Certainly," Bradford said.

Back on the job less than three minutes, and the first crisis was already underway.

If he'd followed his original plan, if he'd stayed away from the Paradise Island Casino, he'd still be in the Bahamas. He'd be out under full sail on the *Southern Wanderer*, taking eight or ten passengers on a casual, aimless voyage through the Caribbean. Louise would be in the galley, overseeing the college students who were preparing a snack for their passengers, and David would be with him up on deck, slowly turning a healthy brown under the sun, learning some things he wouldn't learn in the school Louise had chosen for him in San Francisco.

Now, instead, he was back at this battered, cluttered desk in this aging casino, about to receive his next assignment to protect Charlie Diamond's millions from some hazard, real or imagined.

All because of those ninety foolish minutes at that 21 table.

But there was no going back, no way to erase them. He'd had his chance and he'd let it slip away. And he still faced the problem of talking to Caleb Tompkins, trying to make him understand what had happened, and working out some way to repay the bank's eighteen thousand.

"You've noticed the Monday report, haven't you, Brad?" Diamond asked.

Bradford looked at the papers piled on his desk. "No, I haven't," he said.

Damn it, I just got here. I haven't had time for a cup of coffee.

"Ned Crossley's been studying it. There's something wrong at table seven."

"Is the hold down?" Bradford asked.

It still seemed an odd term to Bradford after fifteen years around casinos: "the hold." It was the percentage of all the money gambled in a casino which the owner kept. For a few of the slot machines—the ones called "liberal pay-out" slots which were scattered around the floor to make the gullible feel that they had a strong chance of winning—the hold might be as little as two or three cents out of every dollar played. But for most of the games in a casino the hold might range from six percent to fifteen or twenty percent and sometimes higher. People who worked around casinos but did not own them sometimes referred to the owner's percentage as "the take," but Bradford had learned early never to use that term in talking to Charlie Diamond.

"Way down, Crossley says. Off more than a third."

Crossley, the executive vice president of the Diamond Mine, had watched over Diamond's money for decades, and he was usually the first one to detect any unexplained decrease in the hold. He was still intoxicated by the sight of all the money flowing through the casino after all these years, and he would often move from one cashier's counter to another, double

checking the count, his long, dry fingers stroking the
bills as he arranged them in neat stacks.

A reserved, withdrawn man, Crossley had a high
forehead and skin like sun-bleached driftwood. He
was eternally disturbed by drafts no one else could
feel, and was always closing doors and windows when
he entered a room. The chill was deep, inside, and was
reflected by his eyes, which were as cold as the surface
of a frozen lake.

Bradford was still searching through the papers
on his desk for the familiar weekly form which served
as a thermometer to measure the health of the Diamond Mine. The reports, prepared by Ned Crossley
and Crossley's irreverent young assistant, Kenneth
Warner, summarized the gross and net income from
every activity in the casino: craps, 21, poker, baccarat,
roulette, the Century Wheel, the slots, the restaurants,
the show rooms, the bars, the gift shop, the cabaret.

"You run across it yet?" Diamond asked, impatient as always about any delay.

"Not yet."

"It must be there."

"It may be, but I don't find it. There's a jumble of
papers on my desk."

Bradford could feel Diamond's silent disapproval
through the phone line. There was never a jumble on
his desk. Compulsively neat. It would be interesting to
trace that back to its origins, to discover why a man
who'd made his living from the disorderly lives of
gamblers for more than half a century insisted on complete order in the world under his direct control.

"Well, get a copy from Ned."

"All right. It's table seven he's worried about?"

"That's right."

"For last week?"

"Especially for last week. But the hold's been down for three weeks running, Ned says. Off fifteen hundred or so three weeks ago, dipped again two weeks ago, and down seriously last week."

"And the table was operating every shift?" Bradford asked.

He raised the question because Ned Crossley still had a bookkeeper's view of the casino. He couldn't understand after all these years why a good pit boss like Chuck Grogan might close down a 21 table for a few hours even if it was scheduled to operate the full shift. Grogan, who was in charge of the area where table seven was located, knew that some players did not like to play head-to-head with a dealer, and wouldn't go to an empty table. In Las Vegas many casinos used shills when the crowd was light, but Diamond had never approved of shills and used them sparingly. Instead, he let his pit bosses concentrate the scattered players during the off-peak hours, even if that left one or two dealers idle for a few hours.

"Every shift," Diamond said.

"I'll try to find out what's going on, then."

"That's young Stevenson's table on the late shift, isn't it?" Diamond asked.

"Yes, sir, it is."

The old man knew that without being reminded. Some people thought he'd lost touch with what was

going on at the Diamond Mine, and it was true that he
no longer had the detailed knowledge he'd displayed
when Bradford first came to work for him fifteen years
before. But once his attention was concentrated on
some activity in the casino he was still capable of absorbing an enormous amount of information in a few
hours. Now that he was worried about table seven, he
could probably reel off a list of the tables in that area
which had remained open, shift by shift, and could
undoubtedly name the dealers at each table.

Diamond had probably observed by now that
Larry Stevenson had built up an unusually faithful
following—men and women who watched for his arrival at seven-thirty each evening and drifted over to
play at his table. Regular customers often had favorite
dealers, just as regular drinkers have favorite bars and
bartenders. The players who returned again and again
to Larry's table seemed to be drawn by the unusual
warmth of his greeting, flattered by the fact that he
remembered their names and attracted by his easy
grin, his boyishly tousled hair, his relaxed, friendly
manner. He was an exceptionally handsome boy of
twenty-one or twenty-two, and he had a look of innocence which hadn't changed since he'd come to
Reno from a small town in Kansas, where his father
was a Baptist minister.

The appearance of innocence—which Diamond
and most other Reno casino owners preferred in their
dealers—could also cause problems. Card cheats—
called "cross-roaders" by many of the older casino

workers—might settle upon a young, inexperienced dealer like Larry as a likely target, assuming that he was too trusting to recognize what they were up to.

"You don't think . . ."

There was the faint hidden stammer again.

". . . some cross-roader has been taking Larry, do you, Brad?"

"I don't know," Bradford said. "Larry's pretty sharp, and I think he'd recognize it if something like that was going on. And Chuck keeps a close eye on all his tables."

"Yes," Diamond said quietly. "Chuck's fine, as long as he's sober."

So Diamond knew about Chuck Grogan's problem too. A pit boss most of his life, Chuck sometimes found the prospect of another shift too grim to face without three or four stiff drinks. Occasionally that became six or seven, and then Grogan looked upon the whole world with a kind of boozy benevolence.

He had the sallow, faintly yellow skin of a man who rarely goes outdoors during daylight hours. His face was puffy and marked here and there by faint blue lines made by broken veins. There were dark pouches under his eyes and a belt of fat around his body.

Concealed by the flab was the young Chuck Grogan who had often run forty or fifty yards down the field on glorious Saturday afternoons, cheered on by the students of Reno High. Once in a great while Bradford would see a reminder of that lost athlete when Grogan moved with unexpected force in expelling a cross-roader from the Diamond Mine. The exertion sometimes left him breathing heavily for an hour afterwards.

Grogan could have gone up to the executive floor during the years when he managed to keep the drinking under control, but he had no desire to leave the world he knew best. He loved the faint sound the cards made when they touched the table, the primitive cries from the nearby crap tables, the triumphant shouts of the winners at the dollar slots, the noise, the tension, the eternal excitement of a casino.

"I believe Chuck's easing up on the drinking," Bradford said, hoping it was true.

"Maybe," Diamond said, unconvinced. "But anyway I'd like you and O'Rourke to concentrate on table seven tonight."

Concentrate.

It was a soft way of phrasing it.

What Diamond was ordering them to do was to spy on Larry Stevenson's table through the eye-in-the-sky, the two-way mirrors which could be found in almost all casinos. Bradford and O'Rourke would spend hours looking down through the mirrors from the concealed vantage points above the casino floor, watching every move Larry made during his shift and every move made by players at his table.

Dealers could never be certain whether someone was walking or crawling along the catwalk above them, or had stopped to photograph them as they worked. In the newer casinos television cameras swept ceaselessly from one table to another, giving security men unlimited twenty-four-hour surveillance. Most dealers assumed that they were always being watched, and many of the casino owners—including Diamond—were convinced that only the thought of those unseen eyes kept most of them honest or at the least severely limited their skimming.

In the Diamond Mine and other older casinos, Bradford had often noticed experienced dealers taking an occasional discreet look at the ceiling. If they saw one of the elaborate old crystal chandeliers tremble, that helped them trace the route of the security man who was making his way along the catwalk, and they would become more cautious in all their movements as he approached their tables.

Bradford heard a soft, dry cough over the telephone. That had begun a month or so before he left for the Bahamas. It was one of the rare signs of weakness in Diamond, a man who had long seemed immune to the illnesses which plague other people. Bradford waited for the cough to end, saying nothing, because he knew that Diamond hated to acknowledge any sign of age and decline, any indication that he would not live forever.

"I hope this has nothing to do with young Stevenson," Diamond said when he'd brought his cough under control. "But he could be signaling his hand without knowing that he's doing it."

That possibility had already occurred to Bradford. An experienced 21 player based his bets partly on his estimate of just how strong the dealer's hand was. If a dealer had an eight or nine showing and something in his expression convinced a player that he had a strong hole card—a ten, a face card, or an ace— that could influence the betting at the table. In the past Bradford had sometimes discovered that an honest but unskillful dealer had given players an advantage over the house because everyone at his table could guess immediately just how good or bad his hand was.

The best dealers revealed nothing, even to the most observant players. They could examine their hole card quickly and casually—whether it was a two or a five, a jack or an ace—without a flicker of a reaction. Younger, less experienced dealers sometimes betrayed their hands by taking a slightly longer look at the hole card if they thought they were about to lose badly, or by some unconscious gesture such as touching a finger to their chins.

"We'll be watching for that," Bradford said.

"It could just be a bad run," Diamond said. But he didn't sound as though he were ready to accept that explanation. After forty years of running the Diamond Mine and some disastrous evenings at some of the tables over those decades, Diamond knew that casinos, like gamblers, had occasional unexplainable runs of bad luck when the cards did not fall right, but he still resisted the thought. "Anyway, take a close look and let me know."

"You want me to call you at home?"

For the past year Diamond's doctor had been urging him to spend more time at his estate on Lake Tahoe and to limit the number of hours at the Diamond Mine. He drove dutifully to the enormous, care-

fully guarded place on the lake at least two or three
nights a week, but when he reached there he settled
down by the telephone in his magnificently furnished
den, phoning instructions and receiving reports. Many
nights he did not go home at all, but spent the few
hours reserved for sleep in his suite above the Diamond Mine.

"Yes, Brad, give me a call. I'll be waiting to hear
what you think."

Damn. It's going to be a long night.

◇

Bradford had just found the last three Monday reports
buried under the other papers on his desk when he
heard the familiar squish, squish, squish of Tim
O'Rourke's shoes.

A tall, abnormally thin man with heavy eyebrows, a waxy pallor and a caved-in face, O'Rourke
had spent most of his adult life on the catwalks in half a
dozen casinos in northern Nevada, finding his way
through clusters of air ducts and huge pipes and
bunched wires with the dexterity of an alley cat. For at
least eight hours a night—often for ten or eleven
when something puzzling aroused his curiosity—he
looked down through two-way mirrors, watching with
extraordinary alertness players, dealers, pit bosses,
floormen, cashiers, and all the other people scattered
around the main floor of the Diamond Mine, his eyes
moving from one gambling device to another, examining every wheel, every table, every slot machine.

The dealers rarely saw him, but they knew he

was there. They called him the "Eagle," and many of them feared his unblinking stare. He could spot a cross-roader more quickly than any other security man Bradford had worked with, and he had remarkable ability in detecting marked cards which had fooled dealers, pit bosses, and floormen.

What made him particularly valuable to Charlie Diamond was his ability to recognize what security men called a "move." A "move" was any unusual action on a casino floor, by a player, a dealer, a kibitzer, or someone just passing through. A player who touched his nose or ran his fingers through his hair or stroked the legs of his trousers or touched the underside of the table might be trying to cheat, and when that happened, O'Rourke became as alert as a pointer. He noticed also when a dealer dealt too slowly (and might be feeding the best cards to a confederate at his table) or too rapidly (and might be dealing from a stacked deck, attempting to reduce the chance of detection by moving the game along quickly). He knew two or three hundred methods dealers had used in signalling to allies at their tables.

One evening O'Rourke noticed that a man at one of the poker tables kept looking at his watch every two or three minutes.

"He knows what time it is," he said to Bradford. "You know why he keeps looking at his watch? There's probably a mirror along the edges of the face, and he's using it to read the hands of the other players."

Bradford went down, asked the player what time

it was, saw the curved mirrors around the watch face, and suggested that the man drop out of the game. He blustered briefly, then sauntered away.

Ordinarily when Tim O'Rourke saw something unusual happening—or about to happen—he phoned down to one of the floormen or the pit bosses with an exact description of the player and what he was doing. But when he wasn't quite sure of the significance of something he'd observed, he would come down to Bradford's office to discuss his suspicions. That was probably why he was here now, Bradford realized.

"Brad . . ."

"Yes, Tim?"

"I know you're busy."

"I am right now, Tim. I just got back a little while ago, and the old man already has me working on something."

"But if you could come up with me for a minute . . ."

Bradford glanced at the Monday reports. The hold on table seven was way down. What he should do next was to dig out all the reports for the past several months, maybe for the past year, and see just when the slide began. If it had started just after he left for vacation, that could mean that others around the casino had decided that this was a safe time to do a little skimming, believing that the whole surveillance system would be a little slack while he was away in the Bahamas.

He should concentrate on table seven, but he knew O'Rourke wouldn't be able to give his full attention to the problem there if he still had an unresolved suspicion in his mind. It would be better to try to clear up this uncertainty first so O'Rourke would be ready to focus entirely on Larry Stevenson at seven-thirty.

"It won't take too long, will it, Tim?" Bradford asked.

"No more than fifteen minutes, maybe less. It might not be anything, but I'll feel better if you take a look."

As they emerged from Bradford's office, located just off the main casino floor, Bradford closed the door behind him. It was probably a good idea to let the pit bosses and the dealers see that he was back, to watch him as he made his way to the catwalk with O'Rourke. If any of them had been tempted during his absence to do a little dipping into Charlie Diamond's profits, this would remind them that the full surveillance was back in effect. He much preferred to frighten the weaker ones into remaining honest, to keep them from trying anything, rather than having to report them to Diamond and Crossley. Once he made a formal accusation against a floorman or pit boss or dealer, the man or woman would be barred from work at any of the major casinos in Reno—and many of them had no other skills.

O'Rourke led the way around the edge of the main floor, where the carpet seemed a little more worn than Bradford remembered, through a dark, unmarked door, up the narrow, winding metal stairs which led to O'Rourke's dusty kingdom.

When they reached the upper level and stepped out onto the first of the heavy planks which formed the catwalk, Bradford paused to glance down through the two-way mirrors strategically placed to give an unobstructed view of all the activity on the casino floor.

He was immediately absorbed with this look at the heart of the Diamond Mine. It was a small crowd—no more than two hundred and fifty people altogether, scattered across the main floor. Two hundred and fifty separate acts of self-deception were taking place as he watched.

A majority of the customers were at the slot machines, and he took a moment to study their faces.

The slots had always been Charlie Diamond's special interest, and he gave as much thought to ways of keeping them busy as he did to all the other activities in the casino put together. He often talked about them, and gradually over the years Bradford had come to understand the old man's fascination with the machines and with the people who devoted thousands of hours of their lives to playing them.

One reason Diamond liked them was because they were completely controllable, completely predictable. By patroling the casino regularly it was easy to detect any attempt to tamper with them, and once they were adjusted by a good mechanic (like Ziggy, who had been with Diamond for forty years) they would produce an income that varied little day by day,

week by week, year by year, as long as there was a
steady traffic of players through the casino. Each machine could be set to "hold" a definite percentage of
every dollar played—as little as one cent out of every
dollar on the most liberal pay-out slots, as much as ten
or fifteen cents on some of the others.

Before Diamond opened the Diamond Mine and
"Pappy" Smith established Harolds Club, most slot
machines were designed and set to hold back as much
as sixty or seventy cents out of every dollar played.
Some offered a sizable jackpot—$150 or $500—but
were rigged so the necessary row of jackpot symbols
never actually appeared. Since the nickels and dimes
of most players disappeared without even the illusion
of occasional wins, many people tried the slots once or
twice, then shied away from them. They walked away
feeling that they had been cheated. Even on the few
honest machines, a player had no more than one
chance in eight thousand of hitting a jackpot, Diamond
told Bradford. Each machine had three metal reels
with twenty symbols painted on each reel. Diamond
figured the chances of the three symbols necessary for
a jackpot being lined up at the same time by multiplying twenty times twenty times twenty—one in eight
thousand. Although the owner's profits from each dollar put into these machines might be sixty or seventy
cents, the total amount being dropped into each slot
was very low.

One night Diamond heard one of his customers
tell a man who had just dropped a nickel into a slot,
"Wise up. You might as well toss your money into the

Truckee as waste it on that damned thing. All you're doing is making the bastard who owns this joint rich. I've never seen that thing pay off yet."

Diamond then asked Ziggy to move three of the slot machines into his office. For three days he spent every free minute he had playing them and never hit a jackpot.

"Open one of them up for me," he told Ziggy. "Let me see how they work."

Ziggy opened one of them and explained the mechanism.

"There must be some way to make them pay-off better," Diamond said.

"More jackpots?" Ziggy said. "That's easy."

Working through the night, Ziggy put three jackpot symbols on the first reel and two on the second reel of each of the machines. He left a single jackpot symbol on the third reel.

Diamond played one of the machines for an hour and won a jackpot. He calculated that a jackpot symbol would now appear on the first reel once in every six or seven plays and one would appear on the second reel once in every ten plays. The single symbol on the third reel would show up once in every twenty plays. By multiplying seven times ten times twenty, he came to the conclusion that a player would now hit a jackpot roughly once in every fourteen hundred plays—almost six times as often as he would on one of the unaltered machines.

Once he'd found out how easily Ziggy could change the odds, Diamond ordered him to work on some slots so they would pay back ninety-eight or ninety-nine cents out of every dollar played.

He then worked with Ziggy in equipping these liberal pay-out slots with loud gongs, bells, chimes, drum rolls and other penetrating sounds and added flashing carnival lights so every player in the casino would feel some of the excitement when anyone won a jackpot.

They experimented with the placement of these machines. Some were put near the doors, others along heavily traveled passageways, a few buried in clusters of lower-paying slots.

The intoxication of sound and light, the promise of $150 or $500 or $5,000 jackpots brought many people back to the Diamond Mine from California weekend after weekend, and many Reno residents got into the habit of dropping in every two or three days. What was extraordinary to Bradford was the slot player's ability to cancel out or gloss over the memory of all his expensive earlier hours with the machines. Even those who won jackpots rarely left the casino with any money, because their good luck on one machine convinced them that they were on a winning streak, and the shower of coins cascading down into the metal pan made them more reckless than before. Yet they were able to convince themselves over and over that this time they would quit when they were ahead: they would take their cups full of nickels and dimes and quarters or their load of silver dollars over to the cashier and turn them into paper money. This time they

would leave the Diamond Mine before they had drib-
bled away their illusory winnings in other slots.

Diamond and the other owners knew that any slot
machine player who stayed in the casino for more than
an hour or two was almost certain to end up losing,
even if he won a fifteen or thirty-dollar jackpot along
the way. The owners could watch calmly as a thousand jackpots were paid during a morning, knowing
that most of that money would never actually leave the
building.

O'Rourke had moved swiftly ahead and Bradford
realized that he had fallen far behind because of his absorption with the slots.

"Where are we heading, Tim?" he called out.

O'Rourke stopped and looked back. "The poker
pen," he said.

"What is it? What's going on?"

"I'm not sure," O'Rourke said, rubbing a bony
hand along the side of his face, feeling the stubble left
from his hurried shave. "One man's up to something,
but I'm not quite sure what."

"How long have you been watching him?"

"About twenty minutes."

"What's he doing?"

"He may have slipped in a marked deck. He
hardly looks at his own cards, then stares at the backs
of everybody else's."

"You can't see the marks from here?"

"No. I've been focusing on the backs with my
binoculars, and I can't see any marks on them."

As they continued threading their way, O'Rourke had to bend frequently to keep from bumping his head on the uneven ceiling, and Bradford followed his lead. They squeezed between huge pipes carrying hot and cold water to the kitchens and the restrooms, and crawled under twisting ducts which drew stale air from the casino floor and brought in slightly less polluted air from the outside. O'Rourke seemed to flow past the familiar obstacles.

"Over here," O'Rourke said.

He was bending over now, looking down through a bank of three mirrors which formed a kind of bay-window above the poker pen.

Bradford crawled through a narrow opening to reach the open space.

"Which dealer?" he asked.

"Trish," O'Rourke said.

Bradford studied Trish, a thin-faced girl with deepset eyes who was flipping cards onto the table expertly. She had once been an excellent dealer, but that was ten thousand games ago. He knew just enough about her personal life to know that it was chaotic. There had been at least three marriages, one of which lasted just nine days, but she didn't bother with marriages now. Instead, she served as support and shelter for an endless sequence of weak, drifting men, all of whom required more of her time and help than her pale, five-year-old daughter, who had already become as adept at survival in an indifferent world as a stray kitten.

Trish's face looked numb now, and Bradford

tried to guess what she had taken to get herself through the shift. Even from the catwalk her eyes had the strained, half-conscious look of someone on tranquilizers.

"Which player?"

"The nervous one, with the brown beard."

Bradford turned his attention to the bearded player. His hair looked as though he had cut it himself, working with dull scissors in a dim light, and his suit was cheap and rumpled. He'd probably saved his money for gambling by sleeping in Wingfield Park or somewhere along the banks of the Truckee. At least he wasn't a successful cross-roader. He was too visible. The best of them had learned how to blend into the crowd.

The man picked up his hand quickly, glanced at it for no more than half a second, then focused his attention on the backs of the cards of the other players. And he was looking at them intently, studying them.

Some security officers would have looked at the man briefly, catalogued him as just another small-timer, and forgotten about him. They would not notice how nervous he was, the slight twitch in the muscles that controlled his upper lip—many amateur gamblers were edgy. And they wouldn't pay any special attention to his stare; gamblers often studied other players, especially at poker tables, watching for any unconscious movement of the face or body or any change in expression which revealed that someone had a particularly good hand or a particularly weak one. But O'Rourke had noticed that the man with the ragged rusty brown beard and the amateurishly cut hair was not looking at the faces of the other players. He was studying their cards.

O'Rourke handed Bradford his twenty-power binoculars. Bradford focused them tightly on the poker table, moving his head as he concentrated first on one set of cards, then on another.

"You see any markings?" O'Rourke asked.

"No, I don't."

"But there must be some. He's been acting like that since he first sat down."

"And Trish looks half-conscious. He could have palmed off a deck on her without her noticing."

"I think that's what he did. He was already in the game when I first came over here for a look."

"You ever see him here before?"

"No, I think this is his first time."

"I guess I better go down for a closer look."

"You want me to come down with you?"

There was no mistaking the reluctance in O'Rourke's voice. This was his world up here. Here he felt at home. When it was absolutely necessary he descended the winding stairs to the main floor of the casino, but he much preferred to report his observations and suspicions to the floormen or the pit bosses or in some cases to Bradford himself. He felt completely alien from those who spent their lives gambling and whenever possible left any direct contact with them to others. He was the distant, uninvolved observer. His attitude toward the players was as impersonal and detached as the attitude of an aquarium visitor toward jellyfish or sharks.

"I don't think that'll be necessary, Tim," Bradford said. "I'll give you a call if I need you, but it shouldn't be difficult to scare him off. Once he knows we've been watching him . . ."

O'Rourke nodded, relieved.

◇

Bradford started back along the row of rough planks that led toward the entrance to the catwalks.

If he were lucky it would all be resolved in a few seconds. A single tap on the shoulder was often all that was needed to send a cross-roader on his way. The ones who had spent years cheating had been spotted often enough to half expect detection. Usually they would shrug their shoulders and head out into the street without an argument, on their way to another casino where they knew the security men were less alert.

Those were the professionals—men for whom this was an occupation with its own clearly recognized hazards. Bradford knew many of them, liked some of them, felt an occasional grudging respect for a few of them.

With amateurs, you never knew. And this one with his cheap suit and crude haircut had the look of an amateur.

Once this was settled, he would concentrate on Larry Stevenson. And tomorrow he'd have to call

Caleb Tompkins at the Reno National Bank and work out some arrangement about the loan.

He should have telephoned soon after he reached Reno. But what could he say to him? How could he explain what had happened to the money?

A man who had never experienced that strange intoxication, when it seems that all the rules which govern the universe might be temporarily suspended, could not understand how that eighteen thousand dollars had disappeared there at the baize-covered table on Paradise Island.

· 2 ·

The Man
in the Poker Pen

Bradford tapped the nervous man with the straggling rusty brown beard on the shoulder.

The man didn't look up.

"Do you have a minute?" Bradford asked him quietly. "I'd like to talk to you."

"I'm playing poker," the man said, his eyes still on the table.

Trish looked across at Bradford, her eyelids drooping from the effects of the tranquilizer.

"Hello, Mr. Bradford," she said in a fuzzy voice, pronouncing his name carefully. "Is there something . . . ?"

It isn't going to be easy.

"I just want to talk to this gentleman here," Bradford said, nodding toward the bearded player.

"Don't bother me," the man said, his voice hoarse and threatening. "I'm trying to concentrate."

"Say, just what the hell's going on here?" the player sitting next to him—a potbellied man with unhealthy purple skin and a broken front tooth—asked, turning toward Bradford belligerently. "Don't you see we're in the middle of a goddamned hand?"

"Sorry," Bradford said. "Finish your hand, and then we'll have to ask you to move to another table."

"Why?" the potbellied man asked.

"Change of shifts."

"Change of shifts, hell. I've been coming here for twenty years. I know when the shifts change."

"All right, all right, let's get on with the game," an old man with a quivery voice said. "You and him can settle things out in the alley later. Christ, a man comes here for a quiet game . . ."

"Go ahead, Trish," Bradford said. "Finish the game."

He backed away from the table and watched as they played out the hand. The man with the rusty brown beard seemed subdued. He glanced at his own hand briefly and without much interest and no longer stared at the backs of the cards held by other players. When the potbellied man raised his bet twenty dollars, he tossed his cards on the table, dropping out of the game.

I came down too soon, Bradford decided. The bearded man was probably cheating, but all I have to go on is O'Rourke's suspicion, based upon a few minutes of observation from the catwalk. I should have waited another ten or fifteen minutes, watching for something specific.

He'd hoped to get it all over with quickly, but by approaching the table too soon he'd lost the chance to discover exactly what the man was up to.

The potbellied man won the hand. He began gathering in his chips while Trish collected the cards.

"You can have your break now, Trish," Bradford said.

"Now?"

The players could tell from her voice that she was surprised.

"Christ, you're back?" the potbellied player said, the purple of his face deepening.

"Take twenty minutes, then go over and help Wanda Jane at the Century Wheel, will you, Trish?" Bradford said.

"She needs help?" Trish asked, looking over toward the elaborately carved wheel.

"Yes, it's light now, but it'll probably pick up in the next hour."

"All right, Mr. Bradford," she said slowly, pushing herself up from her chair. She paused before moving from her chair, raising her hands above her head and stroking one palm against the other. It was a routine still followed at many casinos—a way of demonstrating to the security men watching from the catwalks that the dealer was not walking off with chips

concealed in the palms of his hands. Unfortunately it
was not absolutely reliable. Bradford remembered one
dealer who brought flesh-colored Band-Aids with him
to the table and used them to cover stolen hundred-
dollar chips. He was undetected for weeks because he
had always gone through the palm display so openly
and unhesitatingly.

"I wish to God I knew what was going on here,"
the potbellied man said. "Breaking up a game just
when I finally get a halfway decent hand, a chance to
get back a few of the bucks these cutthroats have been
taking off me."

"There'll be a game starting at the next table in a
couple of minutes," Bradford said. He nodded to the
pit boss who watched over the poker pen and said
quietly to him, "Get another dealer and open table
twenty-four."

"Why are you changing dealers? I liked the one
we had."

"She's taking her break, and then she'll be working at the Century Wheel."

"You still taking in the suckers with that goddamned thing? You guys should be in jail."

Three of the men followed the pit boss over to the
next table. The potbellied man held out for another
minute, then started after them.

"Christ! All this moving around!" he said. "I
shoulda gone to some place where they know how to
run a casino."

The man with the rusty brown beard finished
picking up his chips.

About a thousand, Bradford estimated. Without knowing how much he'd started with, there was no way of determining how much he had won.

Bradford scooped up the deck of cards Trish had left on the table. As he glanced at the backs he could see no obvious marks on them, but he'd decided to wait until he'd reached his office before inspecting them closely.

If he were absolutely certain the man had been cheating he would have ordered him to wait before cashing in his chips. But he had nothing solid to go on here—just O'Rourke's suspicions. If he charged the man publicly with cheating and could not prove it, there could be some bothersome and time-consuming legal trouble, although courts in Reno almost always accepted a casino employee's testimony over the word of the accused.

He followed the man over to the nearest cashier's window.

"After you cash those in, I'd like to talk to you," Bradford said.

"About what?" the man asked, not bothering to look back.

"I just have a couple of questions," Bradford said. "It won't take long."

The man sat in an uncomfortable straight-backed chair, next to Bradford's desk, staring at the floor. He looked sullen and resentful, but not frightened.

Bradford took the deck out of his pocket, held it

loosely in his left hand, and riffled through it twice with his right thumb.

Any crude markings on a deck of cards leaped out at you when you did that. After fifteen years, he could recognize the most common markings quickly. Some cross-roaders whitened out some of the lines which made up the diamond design on the backs of cards used in the Diamond Mine. Others used tiny dots of a daub which was sold in many novelty shops. He could tell immediately that none of the most frequently discovered tricks had been used on this deck.

Next Bradford spread the cards face up on his desk and picked out all the face cards and the aces. He turned them over and studied the backs closely. There was no visible sign of a mark on any of them.

He ran his fingers along the sides of the cards. One unbelievably crude form of marking used by some amateurs involved the use of a soft-gold pin which was attached to the index finger with skin-colored adhesive. The cheater scratched a thin line along the top edge of the cards: one near the top of the card for an ace, a little lower for a king, still lower for a queen. If the light hit the back of the card right, a sharp-eyed player could read the markings by close observation. It was a dangerous trick, and if the bearded man had used it he had undoubtedly gotten rid of the pin and the adhesive after scratching the lines on the backs of the cards. It would be difficult now to prove that he was responsible, even if Bradford found the marks.

While he was holding the cards close to the desk

lamp, looking for possible scratch marks, Bradford realized: *He's not looking at me. He hasn't looked in my direction once since I first tapped him on the shoulder out there. There's some reason why. . . .*

Bradford dropped the cards onto the desk, rose quickly from his chair and stood directly in front of the bearded man. He leaned forward, staring into the man's averted eyes.

There was no question about it.

The eyes were streaked, watery, inflamed. And the man was blinking repeatedly.

"Contacts?" Bradford asked.

The man turned his face away.

So that was why there were no visible marks on the cards. They could be detected only by someone wearing specially tinted contact lens.

I thought they'd given up on those.

When contacts first came into common use, a few of the places that manufactured devices for use by crooked gamblers produced some contact lens that were supposed to make cheating easy and safe. Looking through tinted lens, the gambler would be able to see luminous daubs on the backs of cards which were invisible to anyone else. The problem with those early contacts was an unnatural red color, and for a while dealers were instructed to watch out for anyone who had suspiciously red eyes.

From his brief look at them, Bradford knew that the contacts the man was wearing were tinted a more subtle, natural color—light blue. The card markings were undoubtedly more subtle too.

"Those must have been expensive," Bradford said, still watching him closely.

"I don't know what you're talking about."

For an instant Bradford felt sorry for him. All those weeks of preparation—finding a place (probably in Chicago) which would supply the contacts, ordering them, waiting for them, learning to wear them, then practicing with the marked cards. And once he reached Reno for the trial run: the fear of detection when he substituted the marked deck for the house deck, the discomfort of sitting there at the poker table with the still uncomfortable lens pressing against his eyes, the hostility of the potbellied man while he was winning, the sudden shock of that tap on the shoulder, now the fear of punishment. Something about the crude barbering of the man's hair and the shoddy suit convinced Bradford that he was from somewhere out in cow country, from one of those places where melodramatic stories about people caught cheating in Nevada casinos still circulated: stories about card sharps being taken into shadowy back rooms where men with mallets crushed their fingers one by one, about gamblers who didn't pay their debts being shot through the knees if they were lucky or being buried alive in the desert, five hundred miles from the nearest town, if they were not.

"Where are you from?" Bradford asked him, genuinely interested.

The man stared down at the floor and Bradford was considering what to do next when he muttered through his beard, "Iowa."

"Des Moines?"

"That's right." Surprised, the man looked up. "How did you know?"

"This little trick you're trying here, it's a Des Moines trick."

"I don't know what you mean, trick."

"It would probably go over big in Des Moines, or in Toledo, Ohio. But you're taking a real chance if you try it here."

The man sat silent, again looking at the floor, sullen, mulelike.

Bradford picked up the ace of spades and turned it over.

"I can't see anything on the back here with my naked eye," he said patiently, "but I'd be willing to bet you five hundred dollars right now that I could see a clear marking on the back if I could borrow those contact lens you're wearing. Probably there are dots along the edges which can only be seen if you're looking through lens that are tinted light blue. Or maybe some part of the design of one of the diamonds has been re-traced in some color that I can't see without tinted lens."

"Those are your cards. I don't know what you'll find."

Bradford felt a brief moment of admiration for the man sitting there beside his desk. Caught cold, in a strange town, unable to conceal the evidence which could send him to jail, he was still as defiant as he had been when he was first tapped on the shoulder. Of course, it was the mark of an amateur. A professional cross-roader knew when he'd lost and concentrated on getting away as quietly as possible.

Bradford had a choice about what to do next. He could arrest this trapped stranger from Des Moines and hold him for the Reno police. They would follow his recommendations without hesitation. They would either issue a frightening warning or clap him into the always overcrowded, smelly jail and hold him for trial and almost certain conviction.

If Bradford did ask the police to hold the man, word would inevitably reach Diamond and Crossley. Crossley especially would see it as a sign that Bradford was back on the job, the casino was safe, the trouble at table seven would soon be cleared up too.

It was his decision.

The phone rang.

Damn. What now?

He picked it up and covered the mouthpiece with his hand.

"Let me give you a little advice," he said to the bearded man. "Something like this might make you a couple of hundred bucks down at the Elks Temple in Des Moines, but it could get you shot here. You weren't really cheating the house—we get our money off the top in the poker pen. You were cheating everyone at that table, all the other players. The man with the purple face sitting next to you, the one with the broken front tooth, is probably still wondering why I closed down that table when he was winning. If he asks me, I'll have no choice. I'll have to tell him the truth. You must've seen that he has a pretty nasty temper. And one way or another, word will get around about what you were up to. If I were you, I wouldn't come back to Reno."

"It's a lousy town, anyway. Bunch of hicks here, and half the casinos are falling apart. I shoulda gone to Vegas."

"You know how long it would take them to spot you in Vegas if you tried an amateur trick like this? About ten seconds. They expect to be cheated there, and they're watching everybody who walks in."

The man looked at his watch, his eyes still blinking. "I got a bus to catch," he said.

Bradford looked at him. Ten years ago, he would have held him for the police without hesitating. Five years ago, he would have considered holding him. But now he just thought: poor bastard. Trying in his own blundering, crooked way to stay alive, and just managing. Poor doomed bastard.

"All right, go ahead," he said. "I wouldn't want you to miss your bus."

The man looked directly at him for the first time. Unsure, half expecting to be stopped, he backed out of the office, almost bumping into the wall, feeling his way through the open door.

"Okay," he said, with an uncertain, tentative wave of his hand.

◇

Bradford took his hand off the mouthpiece of the phone. If it was Diamond, he'd be boiling over by now.

"Bradford," he said.

"Mr. Bradford. I'm glad I finally caught you in."

He recognized the voice. Poor Tompkins.

"I'm sorry, Mr. Tompkins. I've been in and out of my office all afternoon."

"You didn't get my message?"

"Your message?"

Bradford saw that someone had pushed back the mound of paper a few inches and had left one slip of paper in the cleared spot. He read the note quickly.

> Mr. Bradford:
> Mr. Tompkins of Reno National
> has called twice. Says it's urgent,
> must talk to you. He'll stay at his
> desk until you return his call. The
> number is 784–2353.
> —K. W.

"Yes, our operator did leave a note about your call, Mr. Tompkins. It was lost in the stacks of paper on my desk."

"I'd hoped you would call me as soon as you reached Reno," Tompkins said.

"I meant to, but things are fairly hectic here. I'll drop by to see you tomorrow."

"Not tomorrow, Mr. Bradford. I need to get this settled tonight."

"Tonight?"

"I'm sorry to rush you, but you must realize that I cabled you that money against all our rules here. Now the executive vice president has scheduled a loan review meeting tomorrow morning at nine, and I'll need to have a clear plan of repayment to show to the other members of the committee if anyone raises a question."

"Why would they raise a question about it?"

"Because it's not secured," Tompkins said, sounding as though he were startled that Bradford did not recognize the implications of that. "A loan of this size—we must have something on paper that shows there's no possible danger of loss to the bank."

"Exactly what do you need? I thought my salary . . ."

"What we need is a specific plan of payment and some kind of security. Although many of the officers do not like to accept boats as security, they may agree in this case, since that's what you used the money for."

"You mean the *Southern Wanderer.*"

"Yes."

"Unfortunately that didn't work out."

"Didn't work out?" The tension in Tompkins' voice was unmistakable.

"No, I planned to buy it when I called you, I thought it was all set, but then . . ."

"What happened?" Tompkins demanded.

"It's a little complicated."

Tompkins brought his voice back under control.

"You mean you didn't need the eighteen thousand after all? You haven't used it?"

"Not for the boat."

He couldn't explain it over the phone. It would be almost impossible to explain it to Tompkins anyway, but it would be better to talk to him face to face, over a quiet drink somewhere.

"You didn't buy the boat, but you don't have the money?" Tompkins said, his voice rising again.

Bradford looked at his watch. Larry Stevenson was due in for his shift in about forty-five minutes. Maybe he'd have enough time to go up to the catwalk and talk to O'Rourke, make sure that the cameras were in place and all the preparations for a complete surveillance had been made, then slip down the street to Harrah's for a drink with Tompkins in the Steak House bar and be back within a few minutes after Larry's arrival.

"Could I meet you in about twenty-five or thirty minutes at Harrah's, Mr. Tompkins? We could have a drink at the little bar down in the Steak House, and talk without being interrupted."

"I can't wait half an hour, Mr. Bradford. I've been here at my desk waiting for your call for an hour and a half already. I need to see you now."

There was no choice. If he tried to delay it, Tompkins would probably come barging in here. He might even call Diamond or Crossley in his desperation—and neither of them liked the idea of Diamond Mine employees owing money to anyone. They knew from past experience that men who got deeply into debt could be strongly tempted by the money they saw flowing so freely through the casino.

"All right, Mr. Tompkins. I'll start as soon as I can."

"I'm leaving my office right now," Tompkins

said. "I'll expect you at the Steak House bar in five minutes."

Bradford heard Tompkins' phone strike the receiver.

He picked up the deck of marked cards he'd taken from Trish's table earlier and put it into the center drawer of his desk.

The bastard with the rusty brown beard didn't realize how lucky he was, Bradford thought. I let him walk quietly away from his troubles. Mine are pursuing me.

He closed his office door behind him and started toward one of the side exits from the casino.

If Diamond happened to pass here and noticed that the door was closed, he would probably assume that Bradford had already gone up to the catwalk and was waiting there for Larry's arrival. Fortunately the old man no longer liked to climb the winding stairs.

On the way to Harrah's, Bradford thought of his opening words to Caleb Tompkins. There must be some way to make him understand what had happened in the Bahamas.

He'd tried often enough to explain such evenings to Louise. She would listen quietly to his story of what had happened at a 21 table at Lake Tahoe after one of his earlier expensive evenings and then she would say, "But you kept betting even though you were losing."

"It was *because* I was losing," he would say. "I couldn't quit when I was so far behind." There was

even a certain logic to it. After an evening of losing
hands it had seemed that it was time for his luck to
change. It had taken him a long time to recognize that
the law of averages was sometimes suspended around
casinos. "Cards have no memories," old gamblers
would say to each other, "Neither do dice." And it was
true, sometimes they fell in your favor all evening,
sometimes they were against you, and the only way to
discover whether they were with you or against you
was to play out the game.

When he watched from the catwalk night after
night, he could recognize how irrational all gambling
was. He saw that even the most analytical and skillful
players won only intermittently. Their inevitable dark
evenings served as a sharp reminder of his own past
defeats.

But then one evening he would convince himself
again that it would not hurt to play a few hands, risking no more than he could afford to lose. Other people
did that and quit. But he was like an alcoholic tenta-
tively tasting one weak Scotch and water. The immunity built up over the weeks or months of staying away
from the table would fail, and he would once again
find himself mesmerized by the cards. The danger of
losing seemed distant and unlikely, the possibility of
an unbroken series of aces and kings, aces and queens,
aces and jacks made it impossible for him to stop.

"Somewhere deep down in the minds of most
gamblers, even the most intelligent, is this completely
illogical belief that the next moment is going to bring

them sudden, unearned rewards, not because of anything they've done, but simply because they want it so
desperately," one of the professors at the University of
Nevada had once told Bradford. "Because that isn't ra-
tional, reasonable arguments will never convince them
they're wrong."

He was talking about me, Bradford realized suddenly. That's what happened that night on Paradise
Island.

Sometimes he would go through months without
surrendering to that strange compulsion. Then one
day he would find himself looking at his monthly salary check and thinking: I could double this in half an
hour.

And because he had had fifteen years to observe
the rhythm of the cards at 21 tables, sometimes it
worked. The chips would begin to accumulate there in
front of him, and he would find himself a thousand
ahead, two thousand, sometimes three thousand.

The real problem was that he could not force himself to stop even when he knew that his luck could
change at any moment.

It was only by accident that he stopped that evening at Lake Tahoe when he was fifteen thousand
ahead. He put off quitting as long as possible, but finally had to cash in his chips because he was overdue
for work.

After he picked up the check for fifteen thousand,
he paused for a moment beside the same 21 table on
his way out. He stood near the player who had taken

his place. The man's hole card was a king, and before the second card was dealt, Bradford knew it would be an ace.

The second card fell. *Twenty-one.*

If he had still been playing, Bradford knew, he would have bet the limit on that hand and added another six thousand to his fifteen.

But how could he explain the impulse that was stronger than logic to a man like Caleb Tompkins?

· 3 ·

An Episode in the Bahamas

Pausing at the door leading into the barroom, Bradford studied Caleb Tompkins' face. He looks a little like my father, he thought. And there's a resemblance in the way he shows his bafflement: the eyebrows raised a quarter of an inch, the wrinkles making deeper ridges than usual in the forehead, the body alert, rigid, waiting. He will probably listen in the same patient way to my story, hoping I can give him some reasonable explanation for my behavior, but not really expecting my answers to be satisfactory. Prepared for disappointment.

◇

"But I still don't know what happened to the money," Tompkins said. "If you didn't buy the boat after all . . ."

His deepset eyes were focused tightly on Bradford's face, his hands pressed flat against the bare top of the table. He looked like a man who was preparing himself for even worse news than he'd already heard.

"It's difficult to explain," Bradford said.

Trying to find some persuasive way to begin, Bradford remembered those few minutes there on the gently rocking deck of the *Southern Wanderer* when he'd managed to convince himself: it's really possible. I can do it. I can make it work.

The first step would be to talk to the owner of the *Southern Wanderer*, find out the lowest down payment he would accept. Then the call to Reno, where he would convince Tompkins that his idea of buying a charter yacht was sensible and that the Reno National would be running no risk at all in cabling him the money. Any other banker would probably say no immediately, but Tompkins knew him, had known him for fifteen years, would remember that he was the chief security officer of the Diamond Mine, a trusted employee of Charlie Diamond, who was probably one of the three or four most important customers the bank had.

Once he'd signed the contract to buy the charter

yacht and made the down payment, he would start looking around Nassau for a couple of vacationing college boys who would be eager to serve as his crew. They shouldn't be difficult to find. He remembered how quickly he had accepted a job like that one summer while he was attending UCLA. He'd choose them because they felt the same way about sailing and the sea as he did. Everybody on the *Southern Wanderer* would be there because they wanted to be there. And they'd follow no set route—sail wherever they felt like sailing, stay out as long as they enjoyed it, return to Nassau when they felt like it.

He strolled slowly around the deck, then went below to take another look at the passenger cabins and the bunks provided for crewmen.

At first Louise would think this was just another of his impractical, doomed ideas. But once she had seen these cabins, rubbed her hands along the oak fittings, seen the small galley and the beautifully designed dining area, stood on the deck with him and David during a soft Bahamas evening, looked down at that remarkable clear water, she would understand that it was possible, and she'd be ready to give him another chance. David was old enough now to race around the decks, and in a few years he could become one of the regular crewmen during the summers.

"I need to know what happened to the eighteen thousand," Tompkins said. "I've never made a loan of that size without some specific advance arrangement about security. The only reason I did it this time was that you made it sound so urgent. You told me that if you didn't act at once you'd lose any chance of buying the boat."

Bradford nodded. That's what he'd said. Could he make Tompkins understand that's what he'd meant? That he wasn't making up a story to get eighteen thousand to gamble away at a 21 table? That there really was an explanation?

◇

He remembered the call to Tompkins vividly.

"Mr. Tompkins?"

"Yes." The voice sounded distorted by distance. "I can't hear you very well. Who's calling, please?"

"This is Don Bradford. Chief security officer at the Diamond Mine."

"Oh, yes, Mr. Bradford. Is this long distance? Your voice sounds very far away."

"I'm calling from Nassau."

"Nassau?"

"The Bahamas."

"Ah."

There was a cautious note in Tompkins' "Ah," and Bradford understood why. To a Reno banker, the Bahamas undoubtedly meant the Paradise Hotel and Casino, and an unexpected call from a depositor in Nassau might mean he'd lost money at the casino and was waiting to be bailed out.

But whatever questions were going through Tompkins' mind, his natural courtesy prevailed.

"What can I do for you, Mr. Bradford?"

"I'm here on vacation, and I've run across a possible investment."

"An investment?"

"It's a charter yacht which is used to take people out on cruises. Room for twelve passengers, a fine galley, a dining area." Bradford realized that he sounded like a salesman. "It's for sale because the owner has emphysema and won't be able to operate it himself any more. I've gone over his books for the past five years very closely, and it's a very profitable boat. It was chartered for twenty-five days last month, twenty-seven the month before."

"You're thinking of buying it?" Tompkins asked.

"That's right. As an investment. He's been charging a hundred dollars a day for each passenger, and even with ten passengers on a cruise he ends up with a clear profit of at least three hundred dollars a day. That's after all expenses, including fuel, food, maintenance, and wages for his crew."

He'd hit the right tone. Tompkins would have been puzzled if he'd told him what it felt like to walk the decks of the *Southern Wanderer* or what the boat looked like under full sail, but his banker's mind could respond quickly to a daily profit of three hundred dollars.

"And how did you plan to buy it, Mr. Bradford?"

"The owner asked for a downpayment of twenty-five thousand, but I've persuaded him to take eighteen."

"Eighteen thousand dollars?"

It was obviously far more than Tompkins had expected him to say.

"Would you hold the line a moment while I check the balance in your account, Mr. Bradford?"

"It's around three thousand dollars, Mr. Tompkins. That's why I'm calling you, to request a loan for the rest. With the boat as security."

There was a pause. Bradford guessed that Tompkins was scribbling a note, asking his secretary to check the balance for him. Those thin, nervous fingers were probably moving rapidly across the notepad.

"I have the figures now," Tompkins said. "The balance in your checking account is $2,911.52." He hesitated. "I could wire you three thousand dollars immediately. That would be no problem at all. In fact
. . ." he'd evidently noticed something else in the file, "you have an American Express Gold Card, I see. We could advance another two thousand against that. Five thousand altogether. I'd think the owner would accept that as a binder, and then as soon as you get back to Reno if you would come by to see me we should be able to work out a loan agreement for the other thirteen thousand."

"That wouldn't work," Bradford said. "Unless I can give the owner a cashier's check for eighteen thousand by eight o'clock tomorrow morning, I'll lose my chance to buy the boat. That's why I'm calling. He's just decided to sell, and I heard about it by accident. By the weekend everybody will know about it, and he'll have no trouble at all finding someone ready to give him twenty-five thousand in cash. If you could see the boat . . ."

Bradford could feel Tompkins' uncertainty over the long-distance line. The easiest solution would be for him to say no, and if it weren't for the Diamond Mine and the importance of keeping the good will of someone who might speak unfavorably about Reno National to Charlie Diamond, that's what he'd probably do. There was a conflict between his caution as a lender and his caution as a banker dealing with someone who worked closely with one of the bank's most important customers.

"Let me do a little checking here, Mr. Bradford, if I can find someone to discuss this with. Where can I reach you?"

Bradford started to say, "At the Paradise Island Hotel," but he knew what that would suggest to Tompkins. A Nevada banker would find it impossible to believe that Bradford had spent no more than ten or twelve minutes in the casino since his arrival in the Bahamas, walking around and taking a look only because he knew that Diamond would ask him a few questions about how the casino was run and how business seemed while he was there.

"I'm not at my hotel now," he said. "Could I call you back in fifteen or twenty minutes?"

"It might take a little longer than that. Why don't you call me in about half an hour?"

"Fine, Mr. Tompkins. And thank you very much."

◇

When Bradford called back, Tompkins asked him half
a dozen questions, obviously searching for some reasonable grounds for turning down the loan.

"You do plan to return to Reno, don't you?"
Tompkins asked.

"Yes, of course."

"Who will arrange the charters while you're
here?"

"The owner has already introduced me to an
agent who's been handling that for him since his doctor ordered him to take it easy. The agent's been char-
tering boats here for twenty years, knows everybody,
takes care of all the details for a flat twelve percent
commission."

"His income depends entirely on keeping the
boats chartered?"

"That's right."

"So you'll have an income from the boat to pay off
the loan, not just your salary from the Diamond
Mine?"

"That's right."

"By the way, what is your salary?"

"Four hundred and fifty a week."

Tompkins was silent for a moment, apparently
making some notes on his pad.

"You feel certain the owner wouldn't accept a five
thousand dollar binder?" he asked.

"Absolutely certain."

Tompkins sighed.

"Well, then, Mr. Bradford, I'll cable you the eighteen thousand. I'll send it through the Bank of the Bahamas in Nassau. You have your passport with you?"

"Yes, I do."

"That should be sufficient identification. If not, call me and we'll work out something to satisfy them. They might want you to tell them your mother's maiden name, something like that."

"Fine."

"And you will come by to see me as soon as you return to Reno, to sign the loan forms?"

"Yes, I will."

"When will that be, Mr. Bradford?"

"I should reach there around noon next Wednesday."

"See you early Wednesday afternoon, then."

"When I telephoned you, I was sure everything was set," Bradford said.

"That's the way it sounded to me," Tompkins said, sipping his margarita. "I didn't like the idea of cabling that amount of money without some clear arrangement about security, but you made it sound so urgent."

"It was," Bradford said.

◇

On the walk back from the Bank of the Bahamas, Bradford decided to take the check directly to John Radner, the owner of the *Southern Wanderer*. There

would be no chance then of someone else hearing the
boat was for sale and making a higher offer. But when
he phoned Radner's house Mrs. Radner said he'd just
gotten to sleep after an exhausting day and that it
would be best for Bradford to see him at the yacht
basin early the next morning. She wouldn't let anyone
else talk to him before then, she said.

After he hung up he considered for a moment the
thought of taking the check by and leaving it with Mrs.
Radner, as a binder. But she'd sounded tired too, and
she wouldn't let anyone else talk to Radner before
morning. Everything was all set.

He ordered a steak dinner and ate it on the balcony while looking across the island to the city of Nassau in the distance. Once the *Southern Wanderer* was
producing a steady income he would find a house over
there—the house he'd promised Louise when they got
married. Or maybe she'd prefer a place on one of the
other islands, safely remote from Paradise Island and
the casinos.

After dinner he went inside and read the thin
Nassau newspaper, watched a scratchy print of an ancient movie on television, drank a Scotch and water,
smoked a cigarette.

He tried to telephone Louise in San Francisco,
but there was no answer. He realized that he didn't
know what time it was in San Francisco.

Bored, he counted the cash in his pocket. Eighty-
nine dollars. He flipped through his remaining trav-
eler's checks. Thirteen fifty-dollar checks—six
hundred and fifty dollars.

He had his return ticket to Reno, and he'd

charged his hotel bill on his American Express card. This was spare cash. He headed for the door.

As he crossed the crowded casino floor, he found himself calculating how high the hold would have to be to maintain the elaborate buildings, pay the staff, and still leave the owners with the rate of profit the huge gambling corporations now expected. In the forest of slots the take was undoubtedly thirty or thirty-five cents out of every dollar played. Since Paradise Island did not have to count on repeat business, there was no reason for them to worry about losing customers by limiting the pay-out. This week's group of blue-haired women would soon be on their way back to New York or London, the swarms of Japanese would be en route to Tokyo, and they would all be replaced by fresh planeloads next week.

The roulette wheels were also probably holding twenty-five or thirty percent. There were only two places in the casino where a skillful player might have some chance, Bradford knew: the craps tables and 21. He'd never been able to join the primitive incantations or share in the peculiar intoxication which was frequently found around dice tables, so he looked around for the 21 tables.

With everything set now, he could afford to play a few hands, even lose four or five hundred.

That was his first thought. But as he started toward the tables, he felt a strange surge of assurance. He wasn't going to lose.

◇

The next card was going to be an ace.

He knew it before the dealer's hands touched the pack. An ace to go with his king.

His bet was one hundred dollars, the table limit, but he should be betting at least a thousand. There was absolutely no doubt in his mind: There was no way he could lose.

It had been three years since he'd last felt that way, one night at Lake Tahoe, and the memory of that session—a fifteen thousand dollar win in less than an hour—made him trust the feeling.

The dealer turned the card slowly.

There it was.

The ace of diamonds.

His seventh win in a row.

But what did it add up to? Seven bets, seven wins, but he'd started betting too cautiously, ten dollar chips at first, then fifties, then hundreds, so he was only a little over four hundred dollars ahead. If he'd trusted his instinct and continued over to a no-limit table, he could be ten thousand ahead by now.

Sometimes at craps, occasionally at baccarat, more often at 21, there was this kind of run which no one could explain. He'd seen it over the years at the Diamond Mine, at Harolds Club, at Harrah's, at places along the Vegas strip. The owners recognized it too as one of the few uncontrollable hazards of their business, the phenomenon they feared most. When it happened at the Diamond Mine Charlie Diamond would deputize Bradford or Chuck Grogan to stand by until the crisis was over, reporting to him by telephone periodically until the player's run of luck ended or the table was closed for the night. He found it too painful to watch himself.

Bradford flipped the dealer two ten-dollar chips as tokes, then gathered up the others. Foolish to waste any more time at this table. This was his night. It had been three years, there had been some costly episodes in between, but it would be foolish to lose this chance.

On the way to the no-limit table, Bradford remembered the Bank of the Bahamas cashier's check, neatly folded in his wallet.

There was an old rule in playing 21: Always start with at least forty times your average bet. If you were planning to bet ten dollars a hand, it was a mistake to begin unless you had about forty ten-dollar chips. Even a winning player had to be ready to ride out an occasional run of bad cards, and if it turned out that he didn't need to use them, the stacks of chips served as a kind of security.

He hesitated for a few seconds, but then he decided. Since he would be betting at least five hundred dollars a hand at the no-limit table, he should begin with around forty five-hundred-dollar chips. Not that he would need them, but it was important to have them in reserve. And he could cash them in along with his winnings after an hour at the table.

◇

Fifty-six golden chips now: twenty-eight thousand dollars.

Bradford pushed one forward, then added another, then another. It was the largest bet he'd made since the evening at Tahoe when he won fifteen thousand.

◇

I've doubled my money.

There's enough there now to make the eighteen-thousand-dollar downpayment on the *Southern Wanderer* and repay the eighteen-thousand-dollar loan from the Reno National.

He had been right about this evening, but still too cautious.

If I'd started betting four thousand each time instead of five hundred, I'd be nearly eighty thousand ahead by now.

Just a matter of moving a few more chips forward a few inches.

He picked up eight golden chips. Four thousand dollars. He pushed them into the circle.

A king and queen. He could double down, but he'd play this one conservatively. With twenty, he was safe.

He glanced at the dealer's card.

A jack showing.

The dealer flipped over his hole card. Ace of clubs.

Bradford watched as the dealer's thin white fingers reached out, drew in the eight golden chips.

Only one way to recover.

He counted out sixteen chips.

The dealer, who had shown no response to his earlier bets, raised one eyebrow.

"Eight thousand dollars, sir?" he said.

"That's right."

He watched his cards fall.

A nine and a jack. Nineteen.

This time he half expected it.

The dealer had a ten and a king.

Although the chill air was moving in waves through the casino, he could feel the sweat beginning to form on the back of his neck.

No time to panic. He had to win it back.

He counted out thirty-two golden chips.

The dealer stared at the stacks for a second or two, started to say something, then decided not to.

Just this one win. Just this one win and then he'd quit.

A five and an eight. Thirteen. If he could get a seven or eight. . . .

A ten.

Bust.

The dealer hesitated a second, then slowly drew in the thirty-two chips.

No, there's no way to explain those ninety minutes at Paradise Island to Tompkins, Bradford decided as he looked across the table at Harrah's Steak House. Especially that final bet when he'd gambled every chip he had left, knowing when he pushed those chips forward that he was going to lose.

It was a gesture he had seen often during his years at the Diamond Mine, the final hopeless bet by a losing gambler. A kind of surrender—the despairing recognition that it no longer mattered, that luck had turned.

A man who had started his working life as a teller, moved slowly up to head teller, then been transferred into the trust department, then promoted to a vice presidency wouldn't understand what had happened at that 21 table.

But he had to try.

"I had been in the Bahamas two and a half weeks when I called you, and I hadn't gone anywhere near the casino," he said. "I went on a fishing cruise, did some sailing, spent hours on the beach. . . ."

After Bradford finished his story, Tompkins took a final sip of his second margarita.

"It's strange, isn't it, that men who spend their lives around casinos develop no immunity? You've heard of Eddie Sahati, haven't you?" he asked.

"No, I don't think I have," Bradford said.

"He and his brother built one of the first successful casinos at Tahoe, just this side of the California-Nevada border. Gamblers who didn't want to waste the time to drive all the way to Reno before placing their first bets would rush to the Sahatis' place from

San Francisco and Sacramento, and it was jammed every Friday night and all through the weekends.

"Eddie and his brother would watch them coming in by car and by bus, see them playing dice or hunched over the 21 tables or in the poker pen, and they couldn't help noticing that after a few hours or a couple of days most of them started back home without a dollar in their pockets. Eddie sometimes loaned some of them enough money to fill up their tanks for the trip back home.

"And you know what he'd do as soon as the weekend crowds thinned out in his casino? He'd jump into his sports car and rush into Reno. He'd bet on anything—fifty thousand dollars on high card. The Smiths were always ready to give him all the credit he asked for, since they knew how profitable the place at Tahoe was. Whatever amount he lost at Harolds Club, they were certain he could cover because of the hundreds of thousands being bet at the lake.

"He had one famous run of luck. One of the Smiths said he won every bet he made for several weeks, and at the end of that time he was supposed to have great bundles of hundred dollar bills in his car—more than a million dollars.

"But then, suddenly, everything went sour. He couldn't win anything. One day Eddie added up his markers and realized that he'd gotten so deeply into debt that he'd never be able to pay them off. He offered the Smiths his part of the casino at Tahoe in settlement of his debt to them. Pappy Smith said no. He was the one who actually ran Harolds Club in Reno and he didn't want to take on the extra job of running a casino at Tahoe."

Tompkins paused.

"What happened?" Bradford asked.

"The Sahatis ended up selling the place to Bill Harrah. He built Harrah's-Tahoe on the land he bought from them.

"But Eddie didn't get enough to cover all his debts. When he died, the Smiths still had an unpaid marker for forty thousand."

Tompkins reached into his pocket for a notepad.

"Now, Mr. Bradford, let's see what we can do. Do you own any real estate?"

"No, I'm afraid I don't."

"Stocks?"

"No."

Tompkins tapped the point of his pencil against the still blank sheet.

"How about bonds?"

"I have a few defense bonds put away somewhere. The Diamond Mine had some kind of payroll deduction plan when I first went to work there."

"How much would they be worth, the bonds?"

"Not much, I'm afraid. Maybe seven or eight hundred. I'd have to check to be sure."

"No more than that?"

"I don't think so."

Tompkins wrote: Savings bonds—$700?

"You do have life insurance?"

Bradford nodded.

"What amount?"

"Fifteen thousand."

"How long have you had it?"

Bradford stopped to think for a few seconds. Nine or ten years? It must be.

Louise had made the appointment with the life insurance salesman. She'd seen the policy as a first step toward changing him into a family man just after David was born. Less than a month later he'd lost three thousand dollars in Las Vegas one weekend, and she had given up her brief illusion.

"About ten years," he said.

"That could have some cash value by now."

"It may have. I don't know."

Tompkins made another note.

"You do own a car?"

"Yes, an MG."

A bachelor's car, Louise called it.

"Paid for?"

"Not quite. I have eight or nine more monthly payments to make."

"Could you bring by the loan papers tomorrow for me to take a look at? I'll need to check on what its resale value would be. Not that we'll have to touch the car."

"All right."

Tompkins made a few more notes, then looked up from his notepad.

"Could you possibly pay four hundred and fifty dollars a month?" he asked. "I know it won't be easy."

"I think so," Bradford said.

He would figure out later how to do it. All he

wanted to do now was to get away from this table, get away from Tompkins, get away from the memory of the disastrous ninety minutes in the Bahamas.

"It's going to take nearly four years at that rate," Tompkins said. "But I don't see how you could manage a higher monthly payment than that, do you?"

"Let me think about it, and I'll let you know."

"All right. I'll have some alternate possibilities ready for you to consider when you come by tomorrow. If you could get by without a car, for example."

"I don't think I could do that."

He reached for the check, but Tompkins moved quickly and held it tightly in his hand.

"I'll take care of this," he said quietly.

And Bradford knew he would take care of it himself, not charge it to the bank.

"Thanks very much," he said.

Almost time for Larry to arrive for his shift. Diamond would assume that he was already up on the catwalk with O'Rourke, waiting. He might have telephoned up to give some final instructions.

"I guess I better run," he said.

"Certainly, Mr. Bradford. Just drop by to see me tomorrow, whenever you have a few minutes free. . . ."

· 4 ·

The Watchers— and the Watched

"God, where you been, Brad?" Chuck Grogan asked. "The old man's been looking for you for the past twenty minutes. I don't know what's bothering him, but I haven't seen him like this in a long time."

"Where is he now?"

"Up there with Tim," Grogan said, indicating the catwalk with a motion of his head. "He's been up and down twice. It's years since I last saw him go up there."

"Thanks, Chuck," Bradford said, racing past him toward the dark, unmarked door leading to the catwalk.

He tried to think of some reasonable explanation for his lateness in joining Tim O'Rourke on the catwalk, but he knew it wouldn't matter what he said. He had been given a specific assignment by Diamond and he had let something interfere with it. Nothing he could say would erase that from Diamond's mind.

Diamond had grown slightly more tolerant over the decades toward the limitations of the replaceable workers who drifted in and out of the Diamond Mine and all the other Nevada casinos: the change boys, the change girls, the keno runners, the girls wearing filmy blouses and brief skirts who served the players drinks, the ancient men who moved soundlessly around the casino floor, picking up scraps of paper, emptying ashtrays and carrying away glasses. Their erratic and disorganized lives puzzled him because anything which was disorderly and unpredictable was difficult for him to understand, but he had learned to expect little from them and to live with their behavior.

He kept a closer watch over those who were farther up the scale, and knew a great deal about them. He knew which of his pit bosses drank too much, which dealers got through the empty days by smoking pot, which middle-aged floormen shacked up with the youngest, leggiest, and most gullible of the keno girls, which security men occasionally spent a night at one of the dismal brothels just outside the city, which employees regularly took their weekly pay checks with them into nearby casinos or over to Lake Tahoe and ended up broke in a few hours. As long as he had precise information about their private lives he was surprisingly tolerant. He believed he could sense it when they grew dangerously bored with their jobs, when they might begin to look around for some way to build up the stake they would need to escape from Reno.

Because he knew of their weaknesses, he had built up an interwoven series of protective layers to detect any attempt by any of them to cheat him. Pit bosses hovered around the tables, watching over the actions of the dealers. Floormen supervised and observed the pit bosses. Security men circulated around the floor, watching over the floormen, the pit bosses, the cashiers and anyone else who handled money. Senior security men like O'Rourke moved restlessly along the catwalks, watching everybody: players, dealers, pit bosses, floormen, cashiers, slot machine mechanics, keno runners, younger security men. Bradford made frequent checks on the senior security men.

All the interwoven spying would seem to make it impossible for any scam to go undetected for more than an hour or two. Yet over the years every casino in Nevada had gone through periods when money was being siphoned off—sometimes a few thousand dollars during a single shift, occasionally three or four million drained away over a year or eighteen months.

Diamond's carefully barbered gray hair, always precisely combed, was mussed now, and there was a dusty smudge along one elbow of his freshly pressed, conservative gray jacket. He was staring down at the casino floor through one of the two-way mirrors, and he did not bother to turn when Bradford approached.

"I'm sorry I'm late," Bradford said. "I . . ."

With a slight wave of his hand Diamond dismissed any explanation. The chief security officer of the Diamond Mine had disappeared for at least half an hour, maybe longer, without even bothering to tell anyone that he was going to be away. And this after he'd received explicit instructions about a serious problem, one that could cost thousands of dollars. Explanations couldn't change that.

O'Rourke, uncomfortable because of Diamond's presence in his small universe, concentrated on table seven with his most powerful binoculars. The camera was set up for filming, but O'Rourke hadn't yet turned it on. He was clumsy in operating the camera, and he didn't really trust it. He spoke with contempt of the elaborate systems in the newer casinos in which some cameras swept endlessly from one end of the main floor to the other and others were trained constantly on the cashiers' counters and the coin rooms. "You still have to have somebody watching the screen all the time or studying all the films," he said. "Why don't they just look down at the floor instead? That way you can see anything that's happening while it's going on."

Bradford moved over closer to Diamond.

"He's not here," Diamond said.

Bradford looked down at table seven. He thought he recognized a few of Larry's regulars, men and women, already gathered there, but Larry himself was nowhere in sight.

He glanced at his watch.

"He's just three or four minutes late," he said.

"Is he usually late?" Diamond asked O'Rourke.

"No," O'Rourke said. "Actually, he usually comes in a few minutes early."

Diamond turned toward Bradford.

"If he hasn't arrived in fifteen minutes, I want you to drop everything and find him. *Everything*. You understand?"

"Yes, sir."

"I have some people coming over to my place at the lake, and it's too late to change my plans. But I'll stay in my office for another twenty minutes. Call me the second he comes in."

"Yes, sir."

He watched as Diamond made his way back along the catwalk.

Diamond would probably never say another word about what had happened tonight, but it would be registered in his mind as long as he lived. And if he ever learned what had taken Bradford away from his post, he might decide the gambling loss in the Bahamas and the eighteen-thousand-dollar debt made Bradford dangerously vulnerable. That would be troublesome even if he were a dealer. It would be ominous in a chief security officer.

Less than a minute before Diamond's deadline Bradford saw Larry Stevenson rushing across the casino floor toward table seven.

Bradford picked up the telephone nearest the vantage point and dialed Diamond's office.

"He's here," he said.

"I was just about to call you, to send you out looking for him," Diamond said. "I'd like to know why he's late."

"You want me to ask him now?"

Diamond considered for a few seconds.

"No," he said. "He'll probably have some plausible excuse. Just watch him now, but just before he goes off shift I'd like you to go down and talk to him and see if he brings it up himself. Don't accuse him of anything, but just see what he says."

"All right. But if he were up to something, I'd be surprised if he came in late. He wouldn't want to take a chance on attracting any special attention."

"You may be right," Diamond said.

Bradford heard one of the soft, dry spasms of coughing which seemed to be coming more frequently now than in the weeks before he left on vacation. He waited until it ended, saying nothing.

"I'll be leaving for the lake now," Diamond said. "But I'd like you to call me if you see anything at all. Even if it's two in the morning."

"All right," Bradford said. "I'll call."

"Did you see that?" O'Rourke asked.

Bradford had seen it. For an instant Larry's thumb and index finger had rested at the top of the waistband of his trousers.

It might not mean anything. But it could explain why the hold from table seven had been low for the past three weeks.

In Las Vegas dealers had been caught concealing chips in many different ways. Some slipped a chip or two inside their shirts, but there was always the danger of the chips sliding out. Others had been found from time to time with carefully constructed cloth or plastic tubes hanging from the inside waistband of their trousers. Periodically during their shifts they would palm a chip and drop it down the tube.

The manufactured tubes were dangerous because they were difficult to dispose of quickly and impossible to explain away if the dealer was searched. In Reno, where many of the tricks used by cross-roaders and casino employees were cruder, a few dealers had come up with a simpler scheme. They attached empty socks to buttons sewed inside the waistband. The sock could be detached quickly and dropped into the nearest rubbish bin if a dealer thought he was about to be detected. Bradford had found two of the socks tossed away so hurriedly that they still contained chips the dealer had not had time to remove.

"See if he does it again," Bradford said.

They watched intently for a repetition of the move, but Larry did not touch the top of his trousers again.

"I don't think that's it," Bradford said after a while.

"No, I guess not," O'Rourke said.

◇

While he concentrated on Larry, Bradford's peripheral vision took in the rest of the casino floor, and everywhere he looked he was reminded of more of the safeguards Diamond and the other casino owners had taken to keep those who worked for them from cheating them.

All the people at the Diamond Mine who handled money or chips were required to dress in specially designed uniforms that made it almost impossible for them to conceal anything. The men's slacks and the women's skirts had no pockets, and the single pocket in the dealer's shirt was always visible to the pit boss, the floorman, and the eye-in-the-sky. That pocket could be used for tokes—the gifts given to dealers by winning gamblers and some losers. Dealers had definite instructions on the handling of tokes: They had to tap the silver dollar or chip against the surface of the table, then lift it above their heads in the direction of the two-way mirrors before dropping it into the shirt pocket, so any security officer in the vicinity could see the size of the toke. Any dealer who received too many fifty-dollar or hundred-dollar chips from the same gambler would be watched more closely.

Because they were required to wear pocketless trousers and skirts, dealers were provided with small cloth purses which they could strap around their ankles. Many of the older dealers refused to wear them, but some found them convenient for carrying their keys, pocket combs, and other small items. Those who used them had to offer them for inspection when they finished their shifts. Occasionally they had to tolerate spot checks when they took their breaks, and it still surprised Bradford how docile most casino employees were about these inspections, which seemed to imply that none of them could be trusted, not even those who had worked for Diamond for decades.

The same suspicion was reflected in the arrangement for handling jackpots. At the Diamond Mine not even the smallest pay-off—seven dollars and fifty cents—could be made by a single employee. A light went on at the slot machine, a low buzzing sound began, to call the attention of players in the area to the jackpot, and a change boy or change girl then used a walkie-talkie to notify the cashier of the number of the machine and the amount of the win. The cashier noted the jackpot on a prepared form and then a supervisor went over to inspect the machine before the seven-fifty was paid. Ned Crossley had held out against all suggestions that the system be simplified for jackpots under ten dollars. That would be too tempting, he said. Sooner or later some of the change boys and change girls would be pocketing some of the money themselves, working with allies who would report a jackpot which had not actually appeared on the machine. There were ways to prevent that, Bradford had argued, but Crossley could not be persuaded.

The men who pushed the hand-trucks filled with rolls of coins and stacks of silver dollars across the casino floor never worked alone, and a series of checks

were made along the way to prevent them from dump-
ing part of the load somewhere with the thought of
picking the missing money up later.

A thousand safeguards had been erected over the
years, yet Diamond and the other owners did not feel
secure. They assumed that some petty pilfering was
going on all around them, and they lived in constant
fear of bolder employees skimming off much larger
sums.

One problem in maintaining full security in a casino was that the people who stole from the owners
rarely felt any real guilt about what they were doing.
After all, they told themselves, the owners themselves
were simply using a more subtle method of stealing
money from thousands of gullible customers.

Bradford remembered the extraordinary scene
when the old Overland Hotel and Casino went out of
business. Although it had been falling apart for years,
the owners were careful not to let anyone know of
their plans until the day the casino was closed. It was
emptied of people early one morning, and almost immediately all the windows and doors were boarded up.

People who knew nothing about casinos probably
assumed that this was just to protect the empty building from vandals, to keep burglars from taking away
the battered furniture and the ancient slot machines.
But it wasn't outsiders the owners were worried about.
They were afraid of the people who had worked for
them. Underpaid, pensionless, offered no severance
pay, left without security of any kind, they were the
ones most likely to turn savagely upon the old build-

ing, strip it of slots, roulette wheels, tables, chairs, lamps, light bulbs.

The owners knew of the smouldering resentment of their abandoned employees. They had no way of answering the angry charges made against them, but they could turn the casino into a fortress—and did.

◇

"You see the one with the moustache?" O'Rourke asked.

Bradford, feeling guilty about letting his attention wander from table seven, looked down. He saw the man now: sick looking, hollow-eyed, moustached.

"Yes," he said. "What about him?"

"Watch him."

Bradford saw the movement which had aroused O'Rourke's suspicion. The man touched his hair briefly with the tip of his index finger, then rubbed that finger across the top of one of his cards.

"Groom and Clean?" Bradford asked.

"Might be."

They had first had trouble with Groom and Clean nearly three years ago. Some cross-roaders had discovered that the hair preparation, which could be bought in many drugstores and supermarkets, was an ideal product for marking cards. When it was rubbed lightly on the back of a card, it made the spot it touched just slightly duller looking than the surrounding area. The mark was so subtle that most players and dealers would not notice it.

Bradford knew there were two great advantages

to cross-roaders in using Groom and Clean. The preparation was used innocently by hundreds of thousands, maybe millions, of men, so the fact that someone had Groom and Clean on his hair proved nothing.
And, even more important, it evaporated within two
or three hours. Even if a pit boss or a security man
happened to catch a man marking cards with Groom
and Clean, it was almost impossible to convict him,
because the dull spots on the backs of the cards would
no longer be visible when the time came to produce the
evidence in court.

   "Maybe we better get some film," Bradford said.
The sick looking man with the scraggly moustache was
repeating the gesture often enough to make a conviction possible before a Reno jury, which usually started
with a strong prejudice against cross-roaders. Bradford
hoped that step wouldn't be necessary. Once he was
absolutely certain he could ask the man to come into
his office and look at the film, and that could convince
him that he should at least move on to another casino.

   O'Rourke adjusted the camera reluctantly, then
waited for the man's next move.

◇

It was all recorded now. Four times since O'Rourke
began filming the man's index finger had moved
to the same spot an inch or so behind his right ear,
and each time he had brought the index finger
down and used it to trace a line across the back of one
of the cards he was holding. It was crude marking,
probably indicating the aces by a line near the top, the

kings by a line slightly lower on the back, the queens by a line just below that, the jacks by the lowest line. As long as this deck remained in play the cross-roader would be able to see immediately whether Larry's hole card was a face card.

"You know, I don't think Larry's noticed what he's up to," O'Rourke said.

Bradford nodded.

That could be the real problem at table seven. Larry didn't *expect* to be cheated. After all, these were his friends. He remembered their names, joked with them, congratulated them warmly when they won, sympathized with them when they lost. At nearby tables the players were intent, serious, sometimes morose. Most of those at table seven were relaxed, good-humored, warmed by Larry's natural friendliness. There was no tension there, and that could be why the man using Groom and Clean had decided it would be a safe place to operate undetected.

"But anyway, the marking isn't helping him," O'Rourke said after another three or four minutes. "He's losing."

Bradford nodded. The man with the moustache had started with about forty five-dollar chips, and he was now down to his last six. He was playing more cautiously now, but as O'Rourke and Bradford both concentrated on him he lost two more bets.

"You think we need to keep filming?" O'Rourke asked.

"No, I don't think so," Bradford said.

There was an unwritten rule Bradford had

learned when he first came to work as a security officer: "Never arrest a cheater when he's losing."

O'Rourke, relieved, clicked off the camera, moved it to one side, and reached for his binoculars.

◇

For a few minutes, Bradford concentrated on another player, thinking he might be a "counter." Many of the casinos had begun to worry about "counters"—players who managed to keep count of which cards had been played from a deck. If many of the tens, face cards, and aces had appeared early in the game, they knew their chances for blackjack had been reduced, and they cut their bets. But if most of those crucial cards were still in the deck late in the game, they often doubled, tripled, or quadrupled their bets, and won heavily when they hit twenty-one.

Although Diamond and Crossley shared the common fear of "counters," Bradford had convinced himself that they were doomed like all other gamblers who followed a system. Their faith in outguessing the house made them vulnerable. Even though they might have a good hour or two some evenings, few of them would cash in their winnings and leave. Sooner or later their losses would cancel out their winnings.

Still, a counter who was having a successful run could account for the fall in the hold at table seven. Bradford watched the one he suspected for an hour, but then decided he was just an erratic bettor, not a counter.

It must be something else.

◇

Bradford watched Kenneth Warner making his way along the catwalk, moving easily under the ducts and past the pipes and bunched wires. Kenneth was lean, fit, and about twenty-four or twenty-five. Bradford had sometimes seen him during his free hours jogging along the banks of the Truckee and had heard him talk about skiing in the Sierra, ambitious hiking trips, and occasional climbs in the most precipitous of the surrounding mountains.

"Hi, Brad," Warner called as he approached. "We've missed your calm hand at the tiller. Good to have you back."

"Thanks, Ken."

Warner nodded to O'Rourke, then asked: "Any idea yet what the trouble is down there?"

"Not yet," Bradford said. "Tim and I have about decided that the man with the moustache may be using Groom and Clean. But if he is, it's not doing him any good. About three more hands and he's not going to have any chips left to play with."

Warner pulled a straight-backed chair over closer to the two-way mirror, turned it around, and draped his long legs casually on each side of it, folding his arms and resting them on the back.

Probably a habit left over from Princeton, Bradford thought.

Warner rarely mentioned Princeton himself, but it was listed on his application, and it had made a strong impression on both Diamond and Crossley. Not many casino owners had Princeton graduates working for them. Warner had come out for the summer after graduation two years before, with the idea of working for a few weeks as a dealer. It would be a diversion, something to talk about when he settled down to the serious business of making a living in New York. A few weeks after he started, Crossley's assistant quit to take a job with MGM-Grand, and both Diamond and Crossley remembered the young dealer with the Princeton diploma. He hesitated briefly when they offered him the promotion, then accepted. Now Crossley depended on him heavily for gathering information about the results in all the games in the casino and helping prepare the Monday reports.

Warner had been watching for about fifteen minutes when he touched Bradford's arm.

"I don't know much about this," he said. "But that man in the leather jacket—could he be an anchorman?"

Bradford picked up his binoculars and trained them on the man with the leather jacket.

He doubted that Larry was working with an anchorman, but Warner was right to consider that possibility. An anchorman served as an ally in helping a dealer fleece other players and the house.

If Larry was using an anchorman, that meant he had either stacked the deck, marked the cards, or worked out some system through which he could read them. The anchorman might have casually placed a shiny cigarette case on the table, making it possible for Larry to read the cards just before he dealt them. If it was a face card or an ace and he wanted to save it for the anchorman, he would then deal off the bottom of the deck to other players.

The dealer would use some subtle signal to tell the anchorman whether he should ask for another card or stand pat. Together they could manipulate a game so the anchorman himself won frequently or so the house won an unusually high percentage of the games. If they were arranging a high proportion of wins for the house, the dealer would then transfer all the excess winnings and some of the ordinary winnings to the anchorman by overpaying him on his winning hands. Players were usually so intent on their own wins and losses that they wouldn't notice another player being paid twice as much as he'd actually won.

O'Rourke, Bradford, and Warner watched closely for nearly an hour before Warner himself said quietly, "No, I don't think that's it."

Warner had returned to his office to check figures from all the activities at the Diamond Mine, then returned to the catwalk a few minutes before the end of Larry's shift. He looked slightly puzzled.

"Anything at all?" he asked Bradford, staring down at table seven.

"No, nothing."

"There may be no problem there. Diamond and

Crossley may be stirring themselves up unnecessarily, like a couple of homely old maids worrying about being raped."

"But the hold has been down."

"No question about that. It was off twenty-one percent three weeks ago, twenty-seven percent two weeks ago, and close to thirty-three percent last week."

"And all the other 21 tables have been doing all right?"

"Yes, most of them have been up from three to seven percent over the same weeks last year."

"And the fall at table seven has been during Larry's shift?"

"That's right. It's always been when Larry and his various relief men have been on."

"What's the situation tonight? Have you had a chance to check?"

"That's what makes me wonder," Warner said, running his fingers through his hair. "The hold from table seven is up by about two percent from the same time a year ago."

"Then maybe it has all been a fluke, what's happened the past three weeks. Other dealers have been through two or three bad weeks through no fault of their own."

Warner nodded. "I'm ready to go along with that, but I wonder if Crossley will? And he's the one who keeps stirring up Diamond."

"Once he has the figures before him showing the results tonight, maybe that will ease his mind."

"Maybe," Warner said. "Unless he assumes that things went better tonight because Larry knew we were watching him."

"How would Larry know?"

"It's been years since Diamond himself came up here, hasn't it?"

"Yes, three or four years."

"Since one of the pit bosses mentioned it to me, I think we have to assume that everybody on the main floor heard about that within about five minutes after he put his foot on the first rung of that damn ladder. If Larry heard about it, and if he has been carrying on a little scam, he would know that this was a night to watch his step."

"But you will be sure to mention tonight's results to Crossley?"

"Oh, sure. I'll give him a call the minute Larry's shift ends. Do you think I should also call the old man?"

"I'll do that. Up two percent at midnight, is that right?"

"That's right."

"You feel fairly sure that this won't satisfy Crossley?"

"I doubt it very much."

"You're going by something he's said?"

"No, he's said very little to me about Larry—he's kept that for his talks with the old man. But I've gotten to where I can guess what's going on behind those alligator eyes."

◇

"Who's that?" Bradford asked.

A girl had just taken the only free seat at Larry's table and Larry was leaning toward her, looking at her hungrily. Although she had to be at least twenty-one to get past the security guards near the doors, she looked no more than seventeen. Fresh, virginal, receptive, Bradford thought—the kind of girl Larry must have dreamed about during those long, hot adolescent nights in Kansas. Long hair, curling softly at the ends, a shy, trusting look, no apparent recognition of the lechery she aroused just by crossing the casino floor and taking her seat at table seven.

"God, how'd you like to step into your shower after a hard night's work at the Diamond Mine and find that eager young body waiting for you?" Kenneth Warner asked. "I thought Chuck Grogan was exaggerating when I first heard him talking about her, but if anything he understated the case."

"Does she come in often?" Bradford asked O'Rourke.

"Every night about this time," O'Rourke said. "Just before Larry goes off shift."

"How long has this been going on?"

"Four or five weeks," O'Rourke said. "Usually she and Larry leave together."

"Hardly able to keep their hands off each other until they get outside, Chuck tells me," Warner said. "That boy's going to be worn out before he reaches twenty-two, with that little filly requiring his attention every night."

"How does she do at the table?" Bradford asked O'Rourke.

"She doesn't win much or lose much," O'Rourke said. "Occasionally she'll win thirty-five or forty dollars, and the next night or two she'll lose about the same amount. Over the past four weeks, I'd guess that she's come out about even, maybe a few dollars behind."

"You've never seen her place a big bet?"

"No. Ten or fifteen dollars is probably as high as she's ever gone."

"What I can't understand is why a girl who looks like that would settle for a 21 dealer. Any high roller in the house would be ready to give her a Jaguar and a house on the lake. I wonder if she's been taken in by one of Larry's stories about the family fortune?"

Bradford had heard echoes of some of Larry's fantasies. He'd told Chuck Grogan that he had an uncle in Argentina who kept writing and cabling, asking him to come down and help run an enormous cattle ranch so he would be prepared when the time came for him to inherit it. He'd told one of the other dealers about an offer of a job in London with an old friend of the family which would require him to spend most of his time traveling from London to Paris to Berlin one month and from Hong Kong to Singapore to Sydney the next, checking on a number of mysterious investments in which another relative was involved—a cousin or an uncle. There were other stories about family holdings in South Africa and Australia. Most of those who heard them soon noticed how vague Larry became when they began asking questions. But maybe the beautiful girl who was leaning close to Larry, their foreheads almost touching, had not troubled him by asking for details.

"I'm glad to see old Larry getting it," Warner said. "He's a good kid, but I still wonder, what's in it for her? Of course, the boy might have some special talents."

"How did he happen to meet her?" Bradford asked.

"Chuck told me that she just happened to come in with some friends after she'd finished her work in the midnight show at the Sahara, and started playing at Larry's table. She let the others go on without her, and she played until Larry was ready to leave. They went off together, and according to Chuck's steam-heated account, Larry hasn't gotten two hours of uninterrupted sleep since then. And he's probably right. Look at those legs. My daddy told me you could always tell by looking at the legs."

"What does she do in the show at the Sahara?"

"You'd think they'd have the brains to feature her, but she's just one of the girls in the line."

Warner touched Bradford's arm.

"I see that Larry has a gentleman admirer too."

A blond young man in his early twenties was watching every move by Larry with total absorption. At first Bradford thought that the man was trying to read Larry's reactions to his hole cards, but then he realized that the man wasn't interested in the cards but in Larry himself.

"The blond man there, third from the right—does he play here often?" Bradford asked O'Rourke.

"Three or four nights a week," O'Rourke said.

"Usually at Larry's table?"

"Always."

The young man had turned briefly to look at Larry's girl. As far as Bradford could judge, Larry was unaware of the small drama there before him. Alert as he was to the mood of the players, he seemed peculiarly blind to some of the things going on around him.

Bradford glanced at his watch. He had seen enough now to report to Diamond, and then the old man might be able to get a few hours of uninterrupted sleep.

"I think I'll give the old man a call," he said to Warner. "Would you mind helping Tim keep watch until I get back?"

"Glad to," Warner said.

Bradford had walked a few steps before he remembered a question he'd meant to ask.

"What's the girl's name?" he asked. "Did Chuck mention?"

"Yeah, he did," Warner said. "Melanie, he said. Very musical."

◇

The phone rang only once before Diamond answered it.

"I'm sorry to disturb you," Bradford said.

"You're not disturbing me. I've been waiting to hear from you."

"We've been watching table seven all through Larry's shift."

"It's not over yet, is it? I thought he had another twenty or twenty-five minutes."

"Yes, he does, but I thought I'd go ahead and call."

"Where are you calling from? The catwalk?"

He could lie about it, but he'd never been good at lying. Diamond had already guessed the answer, or he wouldn't have asked the question.

"From my office. But O'Rourke is still up there watching."

"Well. . . ."

The note of disapproval was unmistakable. Diamond had given him explicit orders to concentrate on Larry through his entire shift, and he had come down twenty minutes early.

"I'm going right back up, but I just wanted you to know that so far we've seen no sign at all that Larry is skimming."

"How about cross-roaders?"

"One man at his table might have been using that hair preparation, Groom and Clean. We have that on film if you think it's worth pursuing, but he ended up losing. I think it would be better to ask all my men to take a good look at the film and then notify me immediately if he comes in again."

"What about the girl who's been hanging around Larry's table? Did she come in tonight?"

So he'd heard about Melanie too. Probably from Grogan; he sometimes stopped by to talk to Chuck, partly to check on whether he was drinking too much. Grogan's own fantasy life was based on his highly colored picture of the steamy, romantic lives of all the younger dealers, cabaret girls, keno runners, and change boys and change girls. His sensual imagination had grown more vivid during the years since his own marriage had fallen apart and with his failure to find any satisfactory substitute despite the opportunities all around him.

"Yes, she's out there now."

"Is she winning?"

"She's making small bets, mostly five dollars a hand. She's about twenty dollars behind right now."

"Has Kenneth Warner given you a report on the hold?"

"He'll be checking again at the end of the shift, but as of midnight it was up two percent over the same night a year ago."

"Up?"

"That's right."

Diamond paused a moment. He had turned away from the phone, but Bradford could hear the distant sound of the faint dry cough.

"You think Larry knows you're watching him?" he asked after the cough subsided.

"I don't think so. At least there's no sign in the way he's behaving. He's been talking to the people at his table, joking with the ones he knows well. If he'd heard anything, I'd expect him to take at least one or

two guarded looks up toward the catwalk. I haven't
seen him do that once during the entire shift."

"If he's sharp enough to take away eight or ten
thousand dollars over the last three weeks, he undoubtedly has enough self-control to keep from looking up at the ceiling."

Bradford waited.

"I want to know more about Larry. And the girl.
What's her name?"

"Melanie."

"Something's been going on at table seven for
three weeks. If they didn't have anything to do with it,
I want to know that. And if they did . . ."

Diamond let his voice trail off.

Now Bradford had his new instructions. Not explicit this time, but definite. He would have to manage
somehow to get into Larry's place and Melanie's, to see
if there were any signs that they had been involved in a
scam. How he did it was up to him. But the old man
would not really rest easily until he had a report on
what Bradford had found.

"All right," Bradford said. "I'll do some checking."

"Thanks, Brad. Sorry you had to come back to
this, but we can't leave things hanging there in the
air."

◇

"Where's Larry?" Bradford asked as he looked down
and saw that table seven was deserted.

"He's gone," Kenneth Warner said.

"Gone?"

"About five minutes after you left. We thought he was just taking an unscheduled break, but just a minute or two ago Chuck Grogan came over and closed down the table."

Bradford reached for the phone and dialed Grogan's number.

"Grogan here."

The voice sounded blurry.

"Chuck, this is Brad. What happened to Larry?"

"He asked me if it would be all right if he left ten minutes early. His girl's gotten a part in a play, and the director has scheduled a morning rehearsal. Larry's gotten used to boffing her three or four times before they go to sleep, and I didn't have the heart to deprive him of his morning exercise."

"But he came in late."

"Yeah, I know. But last week he stayed late a couple of times when one of the other dealers was sick, so I figured he had a little extra time coming. He had a good shift, heavy play straight through."

Bradford rubbed his hand across his forehead. If Diamond heard that Larry had left ten minutes early, that could arouse new questions in his mind. He didn't like any departure from the normal routine.

"Does Larry still have that trailer?" Bradford asked.

"Yeah. Keeps it parked along the river."

"Where?"

"Trailerland, I think it's called. Just a quarter of a mile or so beyond River Bend."

"You think he might be there now?"

"I doubt it," Grogan said. "I don't think his girl would settle for a rumpled bed in a trailer. It's all champagne and silk sheets for her, from what I've heard."

"You happen to know where she lives?"

"Camelot Towers."

"That's a long way from the low-rent district."

"Yeah, I know. You know what they charge for a studio apartment? Four twenty-five a month. Our Larry's found himself a girl with fairly expensive tastes, but I'd say she's worth every penny."

"Thanks, Chuck."

"Oh, sure."

◇

It was too late to do anything more now. But in a few hours he would have to focus on Larry and Melanie. He had hoped a night on the catwalk would give them a clear answer to what was wrong with table seven, but instead it left him with some new questions.

Suddenly he remembered the deck of marked cards he had taken from Trish earlier in the evening. Best not to leave them around.

He opened the center drawer of his desk to take them out. They weren't in the front, where he thought he'd left them. He reached back into the drawer. He didn't feel them. He bent over to take a closer look. Not there.

Odd.

Had he put them somewhere else?

Possibly.

He walked over to the closet and unlocked the door.

Inside was a jumble: decks of cards with every possible marking from crude daubs to the most subtle alterations in the diamond design; dice which had been carefully shaved to increase the number of times sevens or elevens came up; dice with hollow tunnels through which a colorless liquid would flow to increase the number of times snake-eyes or twelve appeared; dice loaded with minute metal weights concealed in some of the dots; magnets which had been attached to a player's belt-buckle or the soles of a player's shoes and then held under one of the old-fashioned roulette tables which could be affected by magnets; a hundred shiny objects, cigarette cases, bracelets, rings, and watchbands which had been used to reflect the cards in other players' hands.

A hundred different ways to cheat. These were the ones they'd found in the Diamond Mine during the past fifteen years. How many hundreds of others had been used without being discovered?

Bradford flipped through a few of the decks of cards on the closet shelves, but he was certain now that he hadn't brought them in here.

He remembered it clearly now: He'd been talking to the man with the rusty brown beard when the telephone rang—the call from Caleb Tompkins. And just before he left for the drink at Harrah's, he'd opened the center drawer of his desk and dropped the pack into it.

Obviously someone had walked into his office, opened the drawer, taken out the pack, then disappeared onto the casino floor.

The man with the beard? Possibly. He had a kind of stubborn pride. He might have waited until he saw Bradford emerge from the Diamond Mine, then made his way back inside to recover his cards. They were carefully marked and expensive, and he would need them if he wanted to try his trick again with the contacts.

But unless he had been unusually lucky in picking his time, O'Rourke would have spotted him immediately from the catwalk. It was one of O'Rourke's most valuable talents—even while he was concentrating on one part of the floor, he seemed able to take in everything else unusual going on anywhere in the casino. After the earlier episode, it was unlikely that the bearded man could reenter the Diamond Mine without being noticed by O'Rourke.

No, Bradford decided, the marked cards must have been taken by someone else—someone who could move casually around the casino floor without arousing O'Rourke's curiosity. One of those he saw all the time: a security man, a floorman, a pit boss, a dealer, a keno runner, one of the skimpily dressed girls who handed out free drinks, one of the gray, anonymous old men who moved endlessly around picking up torn coin packages and emptying ash trays.

Someone they trusted.

·5·

Two Lives

"If you're leching after that one, Brad, I'm afraid I have some bad news for you," Craig Emerson said, leaning back in his seat in the next-to-last row of the darkened theatre. "She's been spoken for."

"It's just a routine check," Bradford said.

Emerson looked at him skeptically. But before he said anything more, he rose dramatically in his seat, his attention caught by the clumsy actions of the stage crew.

"No! No, you fools, not there! Haven't you bothered to watch the play? Alicia has to walk between that

chair and the fireplace, and you'll have her tripping
over Jerome's feet and breaking her pretty ass!"

He waited as the crew moved the chair, then subsided again into his seat. "Worst damned crew I ever
worked with," he said in loud stage whisper which
Bradford was certain carried to the front of the small
theatre.

"How long have you known her?" Bradford
asked, trying to bring Emerson's attention back to
their interrupted conversation.

"Six months, seven months, something like that.
She came here not long after she took the job at the
Sahara and told me in that breathy voice of hers that
she wasn't planning to spend her life as a showgirl. I've
run into that before, and usually the girl turns out to
have vague dreams of someone discovering her the
way they did in the thirties. But not this one—she said
she planned to make her way to New York to spend a
year studying at the Actor's Studio. I suppose she'd
read Norman's book about Marilyn. 'No, my dear,' I
said. 'You're a little late for that. Wrong decade.' Well,
she said, once she got there she would go by to see all
the networks. There were hundreds of jobs in television, she was sure of that. 'Wrong coast for TV, my
dear,' I said. 'Try L.A.' "

"You think she may have a chance in television?"
Bradford asked.

Emerson pushed his beret back from his forehead.
"It's hard to say. There's no doubt about it, they use
up hundreds of interchangeable girls every year. They
have to have them for all those nurse roles, college girls

having abortions, young wives suffering from undiag-
nosable diseases. I have a theory that TV is about to
discover lesbian love affairs, and if that happens that
will double the demand for nubile young girls. They'll
have to come from somewhere and if Melanie can find
a way to stay alive in L.A. for a while and if she's
ready to make herself agreeable to the right people, she
could do all right for a few seasons."

"But that's all? You don't think she has any real
talent?"

"That's a dangerous word, talent. Who can say?
As you know, she's an extraordinarily beautiful girl,
she has a pretty good voice, a little breathy but all
right, she moves easily and naturally, she works hard."

The director paused, seeming to consider the
question seriously.

"She listens intently to everything I tell her—
everything—and then does precisely what I suggest.
Precisely—that's the problem. She talks the way I
suggest, she walks the way I suggest, she has every
gesture right—but she never *becomes* the character. It's
all surface. As I sit out here watching, I find myself
thinking: That's an actress up there, acting."

"Then you don't see much of a future for her?"
Bradford asked.

"I didn't say that. She's very ambitious. It's a
little frightening, that single-minded determination,
and it has carried some very limited actresses a very
long way. A couple of weeks ago I suggested that she
drop by to see a friend of mine who is putting together
a show at the Nugget. Nothing special, but I thought

it would be a small step up from dancing in the chorus at the Sahara. But my suggestion seemed to puzzle her. She wants a career, not a job, and a girl like Melanie doesn't go looking for a career in a taxicab. You fly off somewhere for a tryout, and then, once you've made it, it's all planes and chauffeured limousines from then on. To London for a play, back to New York for an interview on the *Today* show, to the continent for a film, then Broadway. . . ."

"Completely unrealistic?"

"I think so, but I can't be absolutely certain I'm right. There's that extraordinary ambition—that's important. And the body. Not so much the face—you'll find a hundred thousand faces like that—but the way she moves. Any man who passes her on the street has to stop and look. She seems virginal, untouched, but you can't help fantasizing about what it would be like, sleeping with her. That's the magic combination, innocence and passion."

Emerson rose again from his seat.

"You're blocking the door with that table! How can anyone get out?"

He fell back into his seat again as the stage crew rushed to move the table.

"Were you surprised when she began spending so much of her time with a young 21 dealer?" Bradford asked. "I'd think she would have plenty of men to choose from."

"It did puzzle me until this morning, when I heard what he said to her after rehearsal. I think this boy—"

He hesitated over the name.

"Larry," Bradford said.

"I think Larry might be the first boy she's known who is absolutely certain that she will go as far as she dreams of going."

◇

On the way to the bank, Bradford found new questions forming in his mind about Larry and Melanie. If she had now decided that she should go to Los Angeles and wait for a break in television, she was probably realistic enough to know that she would need several thousand dollars to finance her while she was waiting. And Larry's infatuation was probably strong enough to make him take some risks to help her.

It was easy to understand his infatuation. From what he recalled about the boyhood of some of his friends who came from strict Baptist families, Bradford could imagine how hemmed in Larry's adolescence must have been. He'd probably spent his teen years in Sunday school and church and at Young People's Bible Society meetings while hearing other boys brag about their drinking, their pot smoking, and the hours they'd spent in the back seats of parked cars or in the woods exploring the warm bodies of eager girls.

Larry as the preacher's son had probably had no dates at all until he was at least seventeen, and then he'd probably found himself with girls as closely watched as he was—inhibited girls with braces on their teeth, whose mothers had warned them repeatedly about how uncontrollable men were once their animal passions were aroused. Hovering over both Larry and the girls would be the thought of the watchful eyes of Larry's father and mother and the members of his father's congregation, all preoccupied with the sins of the flesh.

It was easy to understand why Larry had stayed in Reno after his discovery of the town on a trip west, when he was heading for California in search of a job.

After all the restrictions of his youth, this must have seemed an adolescent's idea of paradise. Everything concealed or forbidden in Kenniston, Kansas, was offered here freely and openly, twenty-four hours a day. Nude dances, garish massage parlors on the side streets, legalized brothels just a taxicab ride from midtown. Free drinks served by girls dressed in costumes designed to emphasize every contour of their bodies, and he'd probably run into some who were ready to make eager, uninhibited love within a few minutes of their first casual meeting. And gambling everywhere—not just in the casinos, but in the waiting room of the airline terminal, in liquor stores, in barber shops, in supermarkets. It must have startled him at first too to notice that the men and women who came to Reno to join in the revelry included many who would look at home in his father's congregation back in Kansas.

At Reno National Bank Bradford found that Caleb Tompkins had the loan form all made out.

"Take a look before you sign it," Tompkins said.

Bradford glanced at it quickly. Four hundred and fifty dollars a month, first payment due in thirty days. With the money he had been sending to Louise in San Francisco, this would mean that more than half of his monthly take-home pay was committed.

"We could stretch it out a bit more if you prefer," Tompkins said. "I know that's a high monthly payment."

"No, that's all right."

"Well, will you let me know if you run into any trouble?"

Bradford could feel Tompkins' sympathy, and it disturbed him. At thirty-seven, he shouldn't be dependent on anybody's sympathy.

He signed the note quickly, eager to get outside.

◇

He crossed the Virginia Street bridge without thinking about it, and he paused at the sign retracing the founding of Reno. The sign reminded him of the name the Central Pacific Railroad had first given the town: END OF THE TRACK.

They needed some designation for the place on their maps while hundreds of men risked their lives laying the tracks across the Sierra Nevada mountains, and Bradford thought now: That was the right choice.

End of the Track. For the people who spent their lives working at mindless jobs just to earn enough money for their repeated trips to the casinos. End of the Track also for the casino workers who came here with the idea of spending a year or two, saving their money, then resuming their real lives in towns and cities where gambling was still hidden away in pool halls and shadowy bookie joints.

They had heard that Reno was a place where anybody could make three or four hundred dollars a week without bothering to develop any special skills. All you needed to know was how to deal cards and count chips. The money would come from the gamblers, not from the casino owners. Smalltimers would toss over one or two dollar chips after an hour's play, but the big winners and the professionals would sometimes leave a twenty-five-dollar toke, fifty, even a hundred dollars.

The money did come in, but it seemed to blow away without a trace. The year or two stretched out to three, then five, then ten. . . .

◇

It had been a long time since Bradford had last paused to think about this strange town in which he had spent fifteen years.

He remembered something one of the old pit bosses had said when Bradford first went to work at the Diamond Mine. "Remember, this town survives on greed and cunning."

It had sounded harsh and exaggerated, but now Bradford felt that it was true.

From the beginning Reno had only one thing to offer to visitors: Illusion. Although the valley of the Truckee looked green during the spring, the soil was thin and rain was rare. Men coming here in the 1870s and 1880s saw it as an oasis, but that was because they had reached it after crossing a scorched desert of sand, bare rock, and sagebrush. Here they found trees and grass and a bright, clear river fed by melting snow.

Still before them was the great barrier of the Sierra Nevada, where they would face icy winds, treacherous snow drifts, dangerous crevasses, and dark tales of earlier travelers who had survived only through cannibalism.

Here, between the dead lands they had crossed and the frozen mountains still to be conquered, they sought a dreamland, and from the earliest days Reno had set out to create that for them. A false and tawdry dreamland in which a man could drink as long as he could stand, gamble at more tables and more dice pits than he had ever seen before, find hundreds of women who spent their lives arousing and satisfying the passions of men they would never see again.

These earlier travelers moved on to California, taking with them vivid memories of the little western town, the green valley, the sparkling river, the leaves trembling in the wind.

When the gold rush subsided and the caravans west became less common, Reno tried for a while to stay alive without depending on its gambling halls. It was a bleak period. The town began to shrivel and some people feared it would become another of the ghost towns which can be found all over Nevada.

Then, in 1931, it legalized gambling, and the steady stream of visitors returned, looking for the unrestrained world of the old mining towns. Thousands at first, then hundreds of thousands, then millions.

Some began to spend most of their weekends in Reno, returning to California only to earn enough money to finance their hours at the slot machines and the tables. "The dream buyers," a professor at the University of Nevada-Las Vegas called them. Watching them, Bradford understood what the professor meant. As they placed their bets on the slots, at the tables, in the dice pits, at roulette or baccarat, on keno— they *knew* that this time they would win.

When the cards fell, the dice stopped, the reels of the slots came to rest, the wheel ceased turning, they were briefly startled to discover they had not won a thousand dollars, ten thousand, fifty thousand, a hundred thousand. But the shock was brief and the dream was unquenchable.

They would push the chips forward again or put their hands into their pockets or purses for another dollar, another five. They would place the next bet, buy another dream. . . .

◇

Bradford moved his fingers along the highest shelf in the office closet, found what he was looking for, brought it down carefully. It was a dusty plastic case, containing a gift from Eddie Wolfe.

Wolfe had been the chief security officer for the Diamond Mine for nearly twenty years before Crossley had finally persuaded Diamond to fire him. Bradford felt that Crossley's objection to Eddie was based almost entirely on Wolfe's appearance. He was a red-faced man, bloated from thousands of lunches and dinners consisting of bratwurst and potatoes and double servings of desserts, all washed down with many over-sized mugs of dark beer. He had huge hands and huge feet and the chandeliers trembled when he made his way along the catwalks.

Diamond, feeling slightly guilty about giving in to Crossley, told Eddie he could stay on until he'd found a new job. "Just pay me what you owe me up to the minute that bastard made you fire me," Eddie responded with unexpected pride. "I don't need none of your charity."

A few minutes later while he was clearing out his things and cursing Crossley—"that flinty-eyed son of a bitch"—Eddie had reached up to the highest shelf in the closet and brought down the plastic case.

"You may need this some time," he said.

"What is it?" Bradford asked.

"A master key to four-fifths of the doors in Reno," he said. "With these things, it'll be like opening a box of crackers."

Wolfe opened the flap and scattered several items across his desk. The set included screwdrivers, thin chisels, lockpicks and some strips of metal and plastic.

"Take a look," Wolfe said, handing Bradford a miniature screwdriver. "See the workmanship on that thing? And made of the finest surgical steel, all of 'em."

"Where'd you get these?" Bradford asked.

Wolfe laughed. "A little gift from a friend of mine on the Reno police force. They caught me breaking into a poor bastard's house three or four years ago and told me as long as I was going to be operating like a burglar I should at least have some professional tools."

Bradford had never used the tools in the ten years since Eddie gave them to him. But now he opened the dusty case and picked out a miniature screwdriver, two thin chisels, a lockpick, and two plastic strips.

Maybe he'd find nothing at all in Larry's trailer or Melanie's apartment. No marked cards, no stolen chips, no bankbooks recording large deposits, no keys to safe deposit boxes, no notes from Melanie to Larry or Larry to Melanie which indicated that they were working together to fleece the Diamond Mine.

If he searched the places thoroughly and turned up nothing at all, that might help convince Charlie Diamond that Larry was innocent, that the dip in the hold from table seven was a fluke which was now past.

It was possible.

Before morning he would have some idea of Larry's guilt or innocence. Without the search, a shadow of doubt would be hanging over him indefinitely.

The thought that he might be able to clear Larry at least gave him some way of defending what he was about to do.

◇

So this was where he lived.

The frying pan was encrusted with the remnants of the morning's scrambled eggs, the cheap metal coffee pot still contained half a cup of cold coffee, and the metal sink was half filled with unwashed plates, bowls, cups, forks, and spoons. A pair of discarded shorts and two pairs of socks were on the floor near the unmade bed. A pair of trousers had been dropped over the back of a folding chair and a dirty shirt was entangled with the sheets which hung down from the side of the bed.

There were probably five thousand other trailers, mobile homes, and rented rooms in Reno that looked very much like this.

The one permanent characteristic of casino jobs was their impermanence. People came and went, often staying only a few days, more frequently staying only a few months, rarely remaining for more than a year or two. In some casinos the owners had long ago accepted the fact that they had to hire at least four people a year to keep each of the routine jobs in their casinos filled.

Most casino workers were drifters. They'd learned early that if you kept moving you could escape the wearying obligations that restricted most other people. Everything most of them owned could be tossed into a battered suitcase in five minutes, and in ten minutes they could be on the way to the next temporary stopover—Vegas, perhaps, or San Francisco, or New Orleans or Miami.

Bradford remembered what a waiter in the Golden Bowl had once said to him, joking, but still reflecting something of these vagrant lives. "You know," he said, "I was thirty five years old before I knew that when you move on you can take your old lady with you."

The living arrangements of many of the dealers

were as casual and untidy as their rooms. They coupled in the darkness with anyone who was available and uncoupled in the drowsy hours of the dawn, hardly bothering to look back at the rumpled bed as they left to face another dreary day.

Bradford saw a thick paperback book near the single pillow and reached over to pick it up. He expected to discover that the preacher's son from Kansas had read himself to sleep with an erotic novel, and when he looked at the book the title surprised him. *The Rise and Fall of the Third Reich.*

Intrigued, he began examining the other paperbacks scattered around the trailer. A mixture, he saw: *Las Vegas Nights, Catch 22, The Postman Always Rings Twice, Main Currents of American Thought, Fanny Hill. . . .*

On the half-desk which folded down from the wall of the trailer he found two brief stories apparently written for an English course at the University of Nevada-Reno. Odd, no one had ever mentioned that Larry was attending classes there.

Bradford saw the professor's comments on the margins of the sketches and identified him by his initials. He could picture the professor sitting in his book-lined office only a few blocks from the garish world of downtown Reno, trying to understand and encourage part-time students like Larry, casino workers who floated into and out of many university classes, leaving behind them a few half-completed papers, a few hours of their disorganized lives.

Bradford looked around the trailer, deciding where to begin his search.

There was little room for concealment here. It wouldn't take long.

◇

Bradford stood near one of the cars parked on the fourth level of the Camelot Towers garage, waiting.

If there were nothing in Larry's trailer, it didn't seem likely that Melanie's apartment would reveal anything significant either. But Diamond wouldn't be satisfied until he had a report on both parts of the search.

Sooner or later one of Melanie's fellow tenants would pull in and park, then walk over to the door which led out of the garage, across the elevated passageway to the locked door which opened directly into the fourth floor of the nineteen-story apartment building.

If Bradford followed casually a few feet behind, the Camelot Towers resident would probably assume that Bradford was also a tenant in the building and would leave the door open, letting him pass through. With more than three hundred apartments in the Towers, most tenants knew only a few of their closest neighbors and a few people they'd met in the laundry room or the elevator by sight.

Bradford's fingers touched the metal and plastic burglar's tools in his jacket pocket. It was a versatile set, and he could use the lockpick to get into the building if he had to, but that seemed unnecessarily risky. Anyone suddenly driving up onto the fourth level of the garage might see him, wonder why he was hesitating at the door.

Inside, it would be different. Many of the tenants were in their sixties and seventies, he knew, and they would be dozing over their evening television programs. The hallway itself was likely to be deserted and there was little chance of his being observed as he used the lockpick or one of the plastic strips to open Melanie's apartment door.

He heard a car coming up the steep ramp.

It would be a relief when this was over.

The plastic strip was all he needed. It moved easily through the crack of the door, pushing back the latch.

Melanie probably felt secure because the owners of the Towers maintained a twenty-four-hour guard service on the main floor downstairs. She had not bothered to install a police lock.

Bradford glanced at the illuminated face of his watch as he closed the apartment door quietly. Eleven-nineteen. Melanie would be getting dressed for the midnight show, and Larry would be joking with his regulars at table seven, closely watched by Tim O'Rourke.

As his eyes adjusted to the darkness, Bradford looked around. The builders of Camelot Towers had not wasted space. The living room was probably twelve feet by fourteen, but two wide glass doors which opened onto a balcony made it seem less cramped than it would have without the light coming in from the outside. Off to the right was a kitchenette. A rounded doorway led from the living room into a small bedroom, with a bathroom attached.

It was darker in the bedroom than the living room, but with his miniature flashlight he began his search.

◇

He found the passbooks he'd been looking for in the top drawer of the small chest of drawers next to the bed. He brought them out and focused his flashlight on the pages.

The one from the Valley Bank recorded a series of small weekly deposits going back seven months: $15 one week, $10 the next, no deposit larger than $20. The total was $593. If this was her breakaway fund, she still had a long way to go. That $593 would melt away in a couple of weeks in Los Angeles, before any-one in television had gotten around to answering her calls.

He opened the second passbook, from the First Federal Savings and Loan. The account had been opened just five weeks before, and there were four de-posits: $400, $790, $755, $810.

It could be money transferred from other savings accounts, gifts from her parents, presents from some other man besides Larry, fees for modeling. But he didn't think so. This was part of the money from table seven.

In the same drawer he found her checking ac-count records. Most of the income from the Sahara seemed to disappear quickly each month, the largest part going for clothes and rent. The rent had been $295 a month until her move into Camelot Towers, when it jumped to $425.

He pulled out each drawer and examined the contents. He couldn't be certain that all her bank records and important papers would be in one place, but he knew that most people keep such records together. He ran his fingers along the edges and the bottoms of the drawers, looking for a safe deposit box key. Both Larry and Melanie had been in Reno long enough to be aware of the close working relationship between the casinos and the banks. They must know that Diamond or Crossley could obtain information about their checking and savings accounts easily. The only fairly safe place to conceal any large amount of money they had taken from the Diamond Mine would be in safe deposit boxes located some distance from the state of Nevada.

He found no key. Nothing.

Bradford had almost completed his search of the bedroom when he felt something cool and metallic in the bottom drawer of the dresser, concealed under some stockings and pantyhose. He lifted it out carefully, then focused the flashlight on it. A hollow metal cylinder, shaped like a stack of casino chips, with a single five-dollar chip from the Diamond Mine glued to the top.

He had seen several of these cylinders before, but most were rather crudely made. This one had been designed with unusual care and painted very skillfully. Anyone looking at it at a 21 table would think it was an ordinary stack of five five-dollar chips. And during all the movement at a busy table, the chips became part of the background, so it was unlikely that anyone would pick it up to examine it more closely.

It was the simplest kind of cylinder and would have to be loaded by hand and taken to the table. In Vegas some dealers had been caught with intricate hollow cylinders equipped with a spring mechanism. Those cylinders could be placed in front of a stack of chips and would draw four chips in when the mechanism was activated.

With this one, Larry would have to palm some fifty-dollar or hundred-dollar chips during the earlier part of the evening, then disappear into the men's room to load them into the cylinder. Then he would have to take it back to the table and mix it in with the stacks of real chips without being noticed.

Once he had it in place, he would wait for Melanie's arrival a few minutes before the end of his shift. She would bet conservatively, no more than five or ten dollars on most plays, winning some and losing some. Then she would raise her bets so the next legitimate win would result in a win of at least thirty dollars. He would pay her off with the cylinder and at least one genuine chip.

The rest would be easy. She would take the cylinder with her to the women's room, empty it, then go to a cashier's counter which was remote from table seven to cash in the fifty-dollar or hundred-dollar chips.

With one-hundred-dollar chips, they would come out around four hundred dollars ahead each time they repeated the scam. They would have had to use it frequently to account for the total decrease in the hold at Larry's table while Bradford was in the Bahamas. To take in several thousand dollars during those three weeks, they would have had to take repeated risks almost every day.

Bradford turned the cylinder over and over in his hand, considering what he should do. Perhaps just removing it from Melanie's apartment would be enough. When she looked for it in her dresser drawer and discovered that it was missing, that might frighten her and Larry enough so they would take no more chances.

It was a thought, but Bradford knew it wouldn't work. Now that Ned Crossley had played upon Diamond's natural concern over the possibility of being cheated, Diamond wouldn't relax until he knew exactly what had happened at table seven. Bradford knew he would have to show the cylinder to Diamond. Maybe after the first angry reaction he could be persuaded to settle for a warning to Larry—the familiar warning to dishonest dealers to leave Reno and never return.

Diamond put the cylinder down on top of his desk and reached for the phone.

"Send me up a hundred five-dollar chips," he said to one of the cashiers.

When they arrived, Diamond began arranging them in stacks of five.

"Did you see where I put the cylinder?" he asked Bradford.

"No."

"See if you can pick it out."

"Without touching it?"

"Yes. From where you're standing."

"Is it the third stack from the right?"

Diamond touched the third stack from the right and the five chips scattered across the top of the table.

"Remember the trouble they had at the Silver Nugget five or six months ago?" Diamond asked.

Bradford nodded. The Silver Nugget had lost close to two hundred thousand dollars to some crossroaders who used cylinders like this one and some fake hundred-dollar chips which were so expertly made that they fooled the most experienced cashiers in the casino. As usual, the scheme ended when one of the participants felt he wasn't receiving his fair share.

"Have you heard whether they were able to find out where those cylinders were made?" Diamond asked.

"I think they found there were about five places that could produce cylinders and chips that were that good. One in San Francisco, one in New York, two or three in Chicago."

Diamond picked up the cylinder and examined it closely. "Looks almost new," he said. He touched his chin with his right hand, considering what step to take next. "Before we say anything to Larry, I'd like to know where this came from and who bought it."

"All right."

"Begin in Chicago. New York's too far for someone to go to pick it up, I think, and San Francisco's too
close by for them to take a chance. I want to know who
bought it, when, where, how much it cost."

· 6 ·

Something to Fool
Your Friends With

The clerk at the United Airlines counter was used to being questioned by casino security men. He looked closely at the photograph of Larry.

"I'm pretty sure I've seen him," he said. "He live here?"

"Yes."

"I thought so. Where's he work?"

"The Diamond Mine."

"I could have seen him there."

"You don't remember him buying a ticket some time in the past couple of months?"

"Might have. With the number of tickets we're

selling every day now, it's impossible to be sure. I think though . . ."

He hesitated.

"Now, don't hold me to this, because I could be wrong. But I have a dim feeling that he picked up a ticket from me four or five weeks ago."

"To Chicago?"

"That I couldn't tell you. Could have been Chicago, could have been Denver, could have been San Francisco. I don't really remember."

Bradford unobtrusively passed him a twenty dollar bill.

"You don't have to do that," the clerk said.

"You've been very helpful," Bradford said.

"If you'd like to take a look at some flight manifests, I could see if I could dig them out for you."

Bradford considered for a few seconds. If Larry flew to Chicago to pick up the cylinder, he would be cautious enough to pay cash for his ticket and use a false name.

"Thanks, but I don't think that would help," he said. He brought out his American Express card. "Could you give me a round-trip to Chicago?"

◇

There were few passengers on the plane, and Bradford had a row to himself.

He picked at the still half-frozen scrambled eggs and the congealed sausage, then settled for the hot, flavorless coffee.

He opened his briefcase and took out several pam-

phlets from the collection Eddie Wolfe had left in the
desk drawer at the Diamond Mine after he was fired.

He opened the one from Specialty Manufacturers, Inc., in Chicago entitled *1001 Tricks with Cards
and Dice* and read the description of one of their spe-
cialties:

> These Cards Are Not Marked—
> But You Can Read Them!

> It is impossible for the most careful card manufac-
> turer to print the back of every deck perfectly. In every
> pack of cards there are slight differences which pass
> unnoticed even when the cards are used in play in the
> most carefully guarded casinos.

> By taking thousands of packs of cards produced
> by the major manufacturers and examining every card
> closely, watching for these *natural, unplanned, accidental*
> differences, it is possible to assemble a deck in which
> the most knowledgable, alert player can spot the aces,
> the kings, the queens, the jacks, and the tens.

> In the popular diamond design, used in many ca-
> sinos, a perfect diamond shape may occur in the upper
> right hand corner on some aces, while three-quarters
> of a diamond may appear on most other cards in that
> deck. This is normal in the printing and would pass
> unnoticed when the cards are inspected before ship-
> ping. But by examining five hundred or a thousand
> decks, our highly specialized workers would then find
> three other aces which had precisely the same charac-
> teristic—a perfectly shaped diamond in the upper
> right-hand corner.

After assembling those four aces, our workers would then begin searching for an equally distinct *natural* difference on the backs of kings, queens, jacks, and tens. The kings, for example, might have precisely three-quarters of a diamond in the upper right-hand corner, the queens might have half a diamond.

Let us repeat: These cards are unaltered. Every one of them could have been included in a deck sold to any player or any casino. These imperfections would never have been noticed by floormen or pit bosses. All we have done is to assemble decks in which the imperfections will be seen and understood only by the alert purchaser.

These decks are expensive because they are costly to assemble. We call them "sorts" because our workers sort them out from other cards. . . .

◇

"You are looking for some trick cards?" the owl-eyed man asked, looking up at Bradford through his thick glasses.

"That's right."

"To fool your friends with? Is that what you have in mind?"

Bradford nodded.

"I like to clear that up first," the man said. "Some people come in with the wrong idea."

"What idea is that?"

"Well, they hope to use our cards in games where money is bet. They hear that our cards are so good that they would fool anybody, even professional gamblers, and that's what they want to use them for. That's illegal, of course."

"In your booklet, you say some of your cards—the sorts—could be included in any deck sold to the casinos without the pit bosses or dealers noticing anything different about them."

"Yes, that's right."

"You think some people who buy them might try to substitute a deck of sorts during a game?"

The owl-eyed man seemed startled by the directness of the question.

"That wouldn't be ethical," he said.

"Then why do you make that point in your booklet?"

"It's just a way of indicating how good the cards are. To fool your friends with. But if you use them in an actual game where no one knows your advantage over them, it changes the odds."

"In your favor instead of the casino's favor?"

"Oh, I would never advise using them in a casino. No, I wouldn't advise that."

As he looked around Specialty Manufacturers, Inc., Bradford paused at the door leading into the room where women were marking cards. Working under harsh fluorescent lights, they seemed to take artistic satisfaction in the subtle changes they were making on the backs of aces, kings, queens, jacks, and tens. Some were adding a single, almost undetectable dot at a precise spot on the backs of the cards and others were

using a carefully prepared whitener to block out minute sections of the intricate network of lines which
made up the design.

"I suppose these are for amateur magicians,"
Bradford said.

The owl-eyed man nodded.

"I had no idea there were so many of them."

"Oh, yes," the man said, closing the door into the
room where about twenty women were working. "A
very popular hobby."

◇

At the third place he visited he found some hollow cylinders as skillfully made and painted as the one he'd
discovered in Melanie's room.

"How much are these?" he asked the salesman.

"Those? Oh, they're fairly expensive because we
make them to order. You send along a chip and we
design and paint the cylinder to match."

"The chips I use at home, you mean?"

"That's right."

"What if I sent you a chip from MGM-Grand or
Caesar's Palace?"

"Oh, dirty pool! Dirty pool!" the salesman said
with a false booming laugh.

"But you'll design one to work with any chip I
send you?"

"Well, yes, but naturally what we mean is your
own personal chips, the ones you use in games at
home. It's just a trick, you see, to fool your friends."

"Would you show me how it works?"

"It's very simple."

Bradford watched as the salesman reached over and picked up four one-hundred-dollar chips and put them inside the cylinder, which had a five-dollar chip glued to the top.

"A friend of mine bought one of these from you about four or five weeks ago," Bradford said. "You may remember him. About twenty-two, tousled hair . . ."

The salesman's face froze.

"Not me, not me," he said very quickly. "I haven't sold one of these in six months. As I said, they're rather expensive and frankly I wonder whether they're worth the money. We do have some dice I'd like to show you. Some will come up seven or eleven twice as often as ordinary dice, and then we have some that change the odds in your favor just slightly. For a friendly game, of course. But I must say if you could get a pair of these into play at Caesar's Palace without being noticed, they'd never be able to find anything wrong with them."

◇

I didn't handle that right, Bradford realized on the plane back to Reno. The Magician's Warehouse, the third place he'd visited, was undoubtedly where Larry had bought the cylinder, and the salesman with the false booming laugh was the one who'd sold it to him. That sudden frozen look on the salesman's face was as clear a confirmation as anything he could have said.

The mistake was in asking the salesman whether

they could duplicate the appearance of chips from
MGM-Grand or Caesar's Palace. The customers were
supposed to go along with the fiction about the marked
cards and loaded dice and gambling devices being used
just to fool their friends. He should have brought
along a five-dollar chip from the Diamond Mine but
pretended that it was from a set of chips he used at
home.

◇

Kenneth Warner waved to him while he was still
crossing the field toward the ramshackle temporary
structures at Reno International Airport.

"Hi, Ken, what are you doing out here?"

"The old man asked me to come out and watch for
you. You have any bags?"

"Just this one," Bradford said, indicating his small
flight bag.

"Good. Maybe we can get back before Ned or the
old man has a heart attack."

"What's happened?"

"The Century Wheel."

"What's wrong with the Century Wheel?"

Warner, in excellent shape from his daily jog,
moved quickly down the long corridors. Drumlike
sounds echoed all around them each time their shoes
touched the floor.

"Lost $412 Saturday night, $1007 Sunday night,
and $2050 last night."

"That's impossible!" Bradford said. "It's never
lost money since I came to work for Diamond."

"It's never lost money since it was *made*, the old

man says. He's convinced there's only one explanation—somebody's gaffed it."

"How could they? How could they get to it? It's right out in the middle of the floor."

"That's what he wants you to find out."

As he unlocked the doors to his car, Warner said:

"You know, I used to believe that all your troubles disappear if you have fifty million dollars, but after watching our peerless leader these past four weeks, I realize they just get bigger. While I'm waking up in the middle of the night thinking about the rent being due and my next car payment, he's lying awake all night thinking somebody's trying to wreck the Diamond Mine."

Bradford started to report on what he'd found in Chicago, but Diamond was only half listening.

"We'll talk about that later," he said. "We have to find out who's been tampering with the Century Wheel."

He sounded as though he felt the ground shifting beneath him. If he couldn't count on the Century Wheel. . . .

"I'll call Ziggy," Bradford said.

"I've already called him. He's down there now, waiting. I told him to stand by until we come down."

The Century Wheel was visible from every part of the main floor. It rose nearly fourteen feet from the floor and Bradford had often wondered why Diamond's father had insisted on carrying such a monster from one dusty western town to another. Probably because it would be difficult for anyone to walk past it without pausing to look at it, he decided.

Thousands of semiprecious stones and pieces of cut glass had been embedded in the panels of inlaid wood, and the wheel glittered under the light from the nearby chandeliers. Bradford had once heard an old man walking past say, "You know, that thing would look right at home in a fifty-dollar whore house."

Long metal pins extending from the wheel divided it into fifty spaces. A soft leather flap attached to an overhanging wooden frame touched the pins as the wheel turned and the contact between the flap and the metal pins gradually brought it to a halt. The number in the space where the flap stopped determined the winner.

As Diamond, Bradford and Ziggy approached the wheel, four people were playing it. There was a stooped little man who looked as though he hadn't shaved in three days and hadn't eaten a good meal in months, a puffy-faced woman with a shapeless brown hat pulled down over her mouse-colored hair, a woman with blue hair who wore a tight-fitting polyester pants suit, and a man known to every casino in Reno as "Lucky Dan" O'Higgins.

He was called "Lucky Dan" because he almost always lost. What still astonished Bradford after observing "Lucky Dan" for fifteen years was his persistence. He would work at anything—washing dishes, parking cars, cleaning motel rooms, sweeping sidewalks, digging ditches—long enough to earn a few dollars, and as soon as he had collected his day's pay would race back into the nearest casino to try his luck again.

Chuck Grogan had watched him for close to thirty years and sometimes bought him a cup of coffee.

"You've got to realize what his life's been like from the day he was born, that's the only way to understand 'Lucky Dan'," Grogan said. "In the first grade he discovered that he was slower than any other kid in his class and by the time he reached the third grade he knew he'd never catch up. And not just in the classroom—he was hopeless playing baseball or football or basketball too, always the last one chosen for every team. Around eleven or twelve, when boys begin thinking about how they look, Dan looked around and saw that he was the ugliest kid in school too. He knew by then he was dumb, he was poor, he was ugly, and there wasn't a chance in the world that he'd ever be able to do anything more than scratch out just enough money to stay alive.

"Then when he was about twenty-seven, he drifted here to Reno and that first night he went into the first casino he'd ever seen—the old Harolds Club. While he was wandering through there, he saw the lights flashing and heard the bells and the buzzers and the loud bonging sounds. People all around him were collecting jackpots—five dollars, fifteen dollars, fifty dollars.

"He was standing near one of the dollar slots when some poor slob from somewhere out there in

scratch-ankle country won fifty thousand dollars. He'd
won it not because he was smarter than anybody else,
not because he worked harder, not because he'd done a
damn thing but put his last silver dollar into the slot at
exactly the right moment. It was his reward for being a
nothing, a nobody.

"That's what keeps Dan coming back. Some day
he knows those lights are going to begin flashing and
that bonging sound is going to be heard all over the casino, and this time it's going to be for him."

Because it seemed obvious that the wheel would stop
most often on one of the twenty-two spaces marked
with a one, most players began by placing their bets on
that number. In theory the wheel should stop on one
twenty-two times out of fifty, but in fact it stopped
there twenty-four or twenty-five times out of fifty, and
while a player could not win money by staying on the
one he could lose very little.

After several plays on one most players would
decide that the wheel was more generous than other
casino games and they would move on to two. There
were only fourteen spaces carrying that number, but
the pay-off was twice as high: two to one. The wheel
had also been designed in a way which favored the
two, and the players, feeling lucky, would be drawn
on to the five, which paid five to one, then the ten,
which paid ten to one, the twenty, which paid twenty
to one, and finally to the space marked with an American flag, which paid forty to one.

This was the secret of the wheel, Bradford realized. It paid off frequently on the one and the two, but many players soon decided that their chances for a real win would be much greater on the five, ten, twenty, and the flag. Because most players moved on quickly from the one and the two to the higher numbers, the hold on the wheel had averaged thirty or thirty-one percent since the day it had been installed in the Diamond Mine.

"Lucky Dan" had moved through the earlier stages and was now placing his one-dollar bets on the American flag. It was the most certain of all ways to lose money quickly on the Century Wheel, since the flag would have won only one time out of fifty if the wheel had been evenly balanced and actually won only one time out of sixty because of the way the wheel was designed. A player who bet on the flag sixty times would end up with a sure twenty-dollar loss.

"Wait here," Diamond said to Bradford and Ziggy. "I'll be back in a minute."

While they waited, the stooped old man gave up and wandered off, then "Lucky Dan" bet his last three dollars on the flag and lost. Bradford watched him going through his pockets, searching for an overlooked dollar bill or half-dollar or quarter or dime or nickel. Although most people bet silver dollars on the Century Wheel, bets of any size would be accepted. But "Lucky Dan" did not find a dime, a nickel, a penny. The desperate search ended and "Lucky Dan" moved slowly away, slightly dazed.

But he would be back. He would find a temporary job somewhere, busing dishes, or parking cars or sweeping out or carrying a signboard saying "Out-of-State Checks Cashed," and as soon as he could collect his pay for a few hours work he would return to the Diamond Mine or Harrah's or the Money Tree or the Sahara, ready to try again, choosing some game in which the odds against him were highest, certain that this time the wheel would stop in the right place or the jackpot symbols would move into place and the blue lights would begin flashing above his dollar slot.

The hours would pass quickly for "Lucky Dan" even while he was carrying the signboard because of his endlessly renewable faith in all the devices which had been taking his money for thirty years.

◇

The women had given up too when Diamond returned with Ned Crossley, Chuck Grogan, and Kenneth Warner. Three change boys followed them, bringing heavy stacks of silver dollars.

"I'd like to try it for a hundred turns," Diamond said. "Ziggy, you bet on one, Kenneth on two, Ned on five, I'll bet on ten, Brad on twenty, Chuck on the flag. A dollar on each turn."

Diamond took a half sheet of paper out of his pocket and placed it close to the edge of the betting table, which was marked with the numbers one, two, five, ten, twenty, and the flag.

Brad glanced at the neat row of figures, obviously Diamond's rough calculation of the hold he would expect from a hundred one dollar plays on each of the spaces:

Number	Hold
1	$2
2	$16
5	$18
10	$34
20	$20
Flag	$36

The figures for one and ten surprised him. He hadn't realized before that a player could come that close to breaking even by staying with one, or that the hold from ten was almost as high as the hold from the flag. If a player learned of these figures and complained to the gaming commission that the wheel had been gaffed, would the fact that the designer built this distorted pay-off into the wheel more than a century before keep the commission from ordering it off the floor?

They played in silence. During the first ten turns, the wheel seemed to be operating as expected. It stopped on one five times, on two three times, on five once, on ten once. During the next ten turns it again favored one and two, but this time it stopped on twenty. On the thirtieth turn it stopped on twenty again. Bradford's number.

"You're ahead," Diamond said to Bradford, looking at the silver dollars Bradford had lined up.

"Yes, I seem to be."

On the seventy-fifth turn Bradford was farther ahead. While the wheel continued to favor the one and two, it was stopping on the twenty once in every fifteen plays.

Chuck, betting on the flag, lost steadily. On the hundredth turn he put down his final dollar and lost again.

"Betrayed by the flag," he said.

"All right, Trish," Diamond said, reaching out and stopping the wheel as she started to turn it again, "we'll see how it stands now."

Each of them began counting his dollars.

"Ninety-two," Ziggy said.

"That's a little low for one," Diamond said, not bothering to look at the sheet of paper. The expected hold for one was engraved in his mind.

"What do you have on the two, Kenneth?" he asked.

"Eighty dollars left."

"Close enough," Diamond said. "On five, Ned?"

"Seventy."

"That's low, too. Should still have around eighty. I have sixty-six left on ten, which is exactly right. Brad?"

"I'm ahead," Bradford said. "I have a hundred and sixty dollars.

"That's it, then. The twenty."

He moved over to the wheel and touched the panels bearing the number twenty with his fingers. Ziggy followed him, his wild white hair moving with the motion of his body.

"Feel that panel," Diamond said.

Ziggy ran his fingers along the surface.

"You feel a warp there?" Diamond asked.

Ziggy nodded.

"Enough to make the wheel stop there instead of moving on to the two or the five?"

"Not smooth," Ziggy said.

He touched the wheel gently and watched it as it turned. This time it paused briefly at the twenty but then moved on and stopped at the adjoining panel, a two.

"A little work is all it takes," Ziggy said.

"How long?"

"Three hours, maybe. No more than four."

"But how long will it operate the way it should once you've fixed it?" Crossley demanded.

"They turn the wheel too hard, the girls," Ziggy said. "All it takes is a touch." He ran his fingers gently along the ancient surface.

"Damned thing's worn out," Crossley said. "It's at least a hundred and ten years old. Stopping three times as often as it should on twenty now, but next time it could be on the flag. Paying forty-to-one, it could cost us ten thousand dollars a shift before we realized what was happening and closed it down."

Crossley felt no sentiment toward the glittering wheel. He hadn't assembled it and disassembled it a thousand times as a child and helped set it up on a thousand carnival grounds. He hadn't helped conceal it from fundamentalist preachers or rescued it just in time when small-town sheriffs were about to impound it. And he hadn't watched over it for four decades as Ziggy had, always hovering over the ancient cleaning men and women who dusted it, murmuring, "Careful with it, watch how you handle it."

"When did you last take it apart?" Diamond asked Ziggy.

"It was about three months ago. Maybe four."

"Did you notice a warp then?"

"No, there was no sign."

"What we should do is clear this space and use it for five or six dollar slots," Crossley said. "We'd have twice as many players, and the slots would cost practically nothing to operate and maintain. If we set the pay-out at the right level . . ."

"Slots!" Ziggy shouted. "There must be forty thousand slots in town now! But there's not another wheel like this one, nowhere in Nevada!"

"All the others are in museums," Crossley said.

Diamond stepped closer to Ziggy, as though to protect both him and the wheel from Crossley's assault.

"See what you can do with it, Ziggy," Diamond said, touching the wheel gently.

Ziggy nodded, his hair flying.

"Once it's fixed, we should tell the girls not to turn it hard. It's easy." He touched the edge of the wheel gently and the wheel began to move. Bradford watched it until it stopped.

Twenty.

"Again!" Crossley said triumphantly. "You see where it stopped? If someone knew that it was warped and would stop there this often, he could bet a hundred dollars each time and come out thousands ahead. Even if it hasn't been gaffed."

"No one bets a hundred at a time on the wheel," Ziggy said. "I've seen them. One dollar mostly, once in a while a five."

"How have the bets been running, Trish?" Diamond asked.

Her eyes were glazed over. "Different amounts," she said.

"Any large ones?"

"Not large," she said, her voice too furry and vague to carry conviction.

"Once it's fixed . . ." Ziggy said.

"We'll have to see," Diamond said, his voice tired and hoarse. "Rope it off and see if you can take care of the warp. We'll have to test it carefully before we can let anyone play it again."

He motioned to the nearest change boys and they came over to gather up the silver dollars, including the stacks in front of Bradford.

As Bradford waited for a call from Diamond, Kenneth Warner paused in the doorway of his office.

"Old age?" Warner asked. "Or do you think someone's gaffed it?"

"I don't see how anyone could touch it without someone noticing. The damned thing can be seen from any place on the main floor, from the catwalk."

"True," Warner said. "But you could do anything

you wanted to around here between three and five in the morning without anybody stopping you. I dropped by around three-thirty one morning, on my way home from a party, and everybody I saw was half conscious. They were groggy—the floormen, the pit bosses, the dealers, the players, even a couple of your security men. Zombie time."

It was a possibility, Bradford realized. Around three or three-thirty in the morning the artificial tension which kept casino workers and gamblers alert through most of the night began to subside. But there were always a dozen, fifteen, maybe twenty stragglers, like the last guests who cannot bring themselves to leave a dying party. They either had no homes to go to or had no wish to go to the homes they had.

If someone had made careful preparations, he might be able during those drowsy hours to tamper with the wheel. It had occurred to him during Diamond's experiment that it wouldn't be especially difficult to gaff the old wheel. There were thousands of decorative stones scattered all over it, and it shouldn't take long to substitute one or two heavily weighted stones in one of the panels directly opposite one of the two panels bearing the number twenty. The extra weight would cause the wheel to drift down to the bottom of that weighted panel more often than it would ordinarily, and as a result the twenty would win more often than it should.

He should mention that possibility to Ziggy. He would have to phrase his suggestion carefully because Ziggy was still feeling defensive about the wheel. If it could be rigged that easily, Diamond might agree with Crossley that it should be removed from the casino floor.

Warner put his hand into his left-hand jacket pocket, then hesitated.

"I know this is a helluva time to bring this up, Brad," he said.

"What?"

"It may not mean anything . . ."

He brought a torn coin wrapper and some loose quarters out of his left-hand pocket and another torn wrapper and some loose dimes out of his right-hand pocket and placed the wrappers and the coins on Bradford's desk.

"While you were in Chicago, a woman stopped me when I was heading for my office and asked me, 'You work here?' I said I did, and she said, 'What's this about the dimes? Why you charge ten dollars for ninety-eight dimes?' She handed me a package and two handfuls of dimes and I counted them and saw that there were only ninety-eight. But I thought she'd probably dropped a couple of them on the floor, so I replaced the missing dimes and told her that once in a great while the machine which packages coins doesn't function right and that I'd check it immediately to be sure that no other customers would be shortchanged. She seemed satisfied, and I thought no more about it.

"But a few minutes ago I saw a gray-haired couple who come in here pretty often handing some coins back to one of the change girls and I heard them asking her to count them. The man had a roll of dimes and

the woman a roll of quarters. They'd bought them
from the change girl and she had helped them open the
packages. They must have heard a rumor about short
packs, because they began counting them right away,
and both were short. There were two dimes missing
from this ten-dollar pack of dimes and a quarter missing from this five-dollar pack of quarters."

"You're sure?"

Bradford felt a dull ache beginning at the back of
his neck.

"Why don't you double check?" Warner said.

Bradford counted the coins carefully. There was
no question: there was only nine-eighty in dimes and
only four-seventy-five in quarters.

"God damn it," he said.

"I'm sorry to have to lay this on you, Brad,"
Warner said.

"I'm glad you told me."

"I haven't mentioned it to anybody else. I know
what Ned would do—he'd fire all those poor old
women in the coin room and start with a new crew tomorrow morning. No point in adding to the general
hysteria around here."

"Thanks, Ken, for not stirring up Crossley. But I
guess I'll have to tell the old man."

"Today?"

"It's better if he hears it from me than if he gets
the first word from one of those old harridans with
blue hair who spends every afternoon playing the
slots."

"Yes, I suppose it is," Warner said. "You know, they couldn't get me to take your job for a hundred thousand clear a year. Every time you put your finger in the dike to stop one leak, there are fifteen more breaking through."

Bradford picked up the phone on the first ring.

"Brad?"

Not Diamond—Louise. Her voice sounded faint and distant.

"Louise! How are you?"

"I'm fine, Brad. And you?"

"Fine. Fairly busy, but . . ."

They might be a couple of people who had known each other in high school twenty years ago, Bradford thought. Friendly but remote.

"Very busy?" Louise asked.

"Well, yes."

"If you think it would be better to postpone David's visit . . . ?"

Christ! Was that this weekend?

He'd forgotten about it. Completely. Before he left for the Bahamas they had chosen four weekends, all carefully worked out so that David wouldn't forget that he had a father.

"No, no, this weekend will be fine."

"Good," Louise said. "He's been talking about it every day for the past two weeks, counting the days until his flight. I discovered this morning that he'd marked it down on the kitchen calendar. He drew stars in the spaces for this Saturday and Sunday and he wrote in capital letters—'Dad' and 'Reno'."

"I'll meet his plane," Bradford said. "Which flight will he be on?"

"United, arriving at nine-thirty Saturday morning. I'll check the flight number."

"Don't bother. As long as I know the time. I'll be waiting."

"I'm glad you won't have to postpone it, Brad. I was afraid you might be too busy to spend any time with him, and he would have been so disappointed."

"It'll be good to have him here. I'll make the time."

The question was how. . . .

◇

As soon as he put the phone down, it rang again.

"Brad?"

"Yes, sir."

"We have found something. I don't know exactly what it means, but we better have a talk. Could you come up?"

"Be right up."

Diamond was holding a blue stone in his hand when Bradford entered his office.

He handed it to Bradford. It felt heavy, weighted.

"Was this on the Century Wheel?" Bradford asked.

"No, not on the wheel. It was in a wastebasket about ten feet away. One of the cleaning men found it and gave it to Kenneth."

"If it wasn't on the wheel . . . ?"

"Why would somebody weight it?" Diamond asked. "I don't know if they'd actually used it, but they must have had some reason for having it ready."

Bradford looked at it. Examined closely, the weighting with metal was obvious. But of course if someone had concealed it among all the false stones on the Century Wheel no one would have bothered to look at it closely.

"I just don't understand what it means," Bradford said. "If somebody meant to use this on the wheel, I think we'd have caught him. Even if no one on the main floor noticed him, Tim or one of the other men on the catwalk would have seen him removing another stone and gluing on this one. With everything that's been happening here . . ."

"It's still happening, isn't it, Brad?" Diamond said. "I hoped when you came back . . ."

It was a terrible time to bring up another problem, Bradford realized, but he felt he had no choice. If he delayed telling Diamond about the customers' complaints, Diamond would consider it an act of deception, and he'd be right.

"There's some trouble in the coin room too," Bradford said.

Diamond looked as though he'd been hit with a baseball bat.

"What did you say?" he asked, his voice hoarser than before.

"I don't know how serious it is, but two or three customers have complained that coin rolls were short."

"Complained to you?"

"No, to Kenneth."

"When?"

"Just before I came up."

He'd already decided that it would be better not to mention that Kenneth had kept this information to himself while waiting for Bradford to return from Chicago. Delaying a warning about any possible scam in the coin room or the counting room was as dangerous as delaying a fire alarm.

Diamond must be thinking about the revelation a year earlier that an alliance of casino employees in Las Vegas had made off with at least three million dollars by short-packaging every roll of coins sold to the casino's customers. Few had noticed, since most slot machine players are so impatient about getting to their favorite machines that they do not bother to count their coins. The occasional customer who did complain was quickly pacified by someone involved in the scam, which included change boys and change girls as well as people working in the coin room, cashiers, and some of the executives. The skimming might have continued indefinitely, but after eighteen months one of the group reported it to the gaming commission because he felt he wasn't getting his fair share.

Diamond supported his head with his hand, leaning over his desk.

"Table seven, the Century Wheel, now the coin room," he said. "Where are they going to show up next, Brad?"

They.

The word had been hovering there in the air, but it was the first time Diamond had used it.

He was no longer thinking of some minor, isolated scam operated by Larry and Melanie or another scheme involving a player who had found a way to make two or three thousand dollars on the Century Wheel. Instead he had moved on to imagining some dangerous, shadowy group which had chosen the Diamond Mine as its target. Crossley had succeeded in convincing him that he was the victim of the most deadly of all threats to a casino—a wide-ranging, insidious scam carried out by people who understood exactly how a gambling enterprise worked and how vulnerable it was.

"I'm not sure yet what the problem is there," Bradford said.

"How many complaints?"

"Only three."

"Just three who bothered to count their coins," Diamond said. "Hundreds could have been shortchanged. Or more."

"I'll set up a spot check immediately."

"Put everyone you need on it. Use some of the keno girls. I want an exact count of every hundredth roll that comes out of the coin room."

"All right."

"No—make that every fiftieth roll. And tell them in the coin room that we'll be checking on them indefinitely. If someone complained to the gaming commission . . ."

That was the darkest shadow yet. If a customer believed he was being cheated in a Nevada casino, he could demand that the gaming commission send in agents to carry out an unannounced spot check. Gaming-board agents had the authority to halt any game and to order dealers to turn over the cards or stickmen to surrender the dice. If a few customers complained that they had been short-changed, the agents could paralyze the casino by ordering that every roll be opened and counted before it could be sold. Although it rarely used it, the gaming board had the power to close down a casino indefinitely or even order the sale of the casino to other owners and operators.

"I don't think there's much chance of that," Bradford said.

Diamond walked over and looked out the window. At least a hundred and fifty tourists had just been unloaded from tour busses and he watched to see how many were going into Harrah's Club, how many into Fitzgerald's, how many into Harolds, how many were heading toward the Diamond Mine.

"Once a report like this gets around, it can make thousands of players pass us by," Diamond said. "It's like a hemorrhage. We have to stop it immediately."

"I'll get right to it."

Diamond nodded. "Later I'd like to hear about

what you found in Chicago. Do you know which place the cylinder came from?"

"I'm almost certain it came from a place called the Magician's Warehouse."

"What did it cost?"

"The salesman I talked to just said they were fairly expensive. Because they have to be individually made and painted, I'd estimate that it would be somewhere around two hundred and fifty dollars, maybe three hundred."

The cough began. Deeper than before, it shook Diamond's body and Bradford noticed for the first time how pale he looked.

The sound continued for almost a minute, and when it ended finally Diamond said no more. As Bradford started out of the office, Diamond sank into his elaborately carved chair, looking weary and defeated.

The crudely weighted blue stone was there on his desk, a reminder of all the unanswered questions.

· 7 ·

Death
in the Mountains

"You sure you'll be all right here for a few minutes, David?" Bradford asked.

"Sure, Dad. I'll be fine."

Bradford looked around the children's floor of Circus-Circus, realizing for the first time how skillfully the owners had duplicated the appeal of a casino while remaining just inside the law. No one under twenty-one could be admitted to the crowded gambling floor one flight down, but here on this level there were the same penetrating sounds and flash of lights when boys and girls, some only four or five years old, won cheap toys by playing various carnival games. A juvenile casino, preparing a new generation for the time when they would move from galleries where they were shooting at ducks to win a stuffed dog to putting their coins in the slot machines and their dollars on the 21 tables.

At the Diamond Mine and other older casinos where little or no provision was made to keep the children occupied while their parents were at the tables or the slots, it was still common to see kids standing just outside the doors of the casinos, waiting. The sounds of the coins hitting the metal pans and the bells and the chimes and the buzzers told them that something extraordinary was happening there, but that for some reason only their parents could play these games. They were barred.

One evening when Kenneth Warner had worked until almost midnight he found a boy of five and a girl of three curled up in the corner of the open doorway, asleep. Warner, who rarely showed any emotion, went back in, carrying the girl and holding the boy's hand, asking customer after customer, "Did you leave these children out there?"

"You can't bring the children inside," one of Bradford's security guards told Warner.

"Then find their parents!" Warner said. "Find them and bring them here!"

Bradford had wondered later whether the sight of the abandoned children had reminded Warner of something in his childhood.

"I won't be gone long," Bradford said. "Maybe half an hour, no more."

"Don't rush, Dad. I'll be okay."

David was looking at him, unblinking, but Bradford tried to imagine what was going on behind the boy's solemn brown eyes. By the time he was four David had learned not to reveal too much of what he was feeling. And he had developed a habit of searching Bradford's face, as though he were trying to discover the real meaning behind his father's words. Bradford still remembered waking up early one morning and seeing David's face only a few inches from his own, those brown eyes studying him intently.

"This is your day, David, once I clear up a couple of things at the office. Where'd you like to go?"

"It doesn't matter, Dad. Wherever you'd like."

There was a slight hesitation in his voice, almost a stammer. Bradford had never noticed that before. It suddenly struck him—it was the same kind of occasional hesitation that Charlie Diamond had, a consequence of the fears and uncertainties of his childhood.

David's first ten years had been far less unsettled, but it was easy to understand how the sudden move from Reno to San Francisco, with his father remaining in Reno, could have left him slightly shaken, no longer able to believe that there would always be a small part of the universe that would remain stable, unchanged, regardless of what happened.

Suddenly, perhaps because of his vivid memory of children left in casino doorways, moved by the solemnity of David's expression, Bradford heard himself saying, "I saw a boat while I was in the Bahamas, one you'd like. I was thinking I might buy it and then you and I and your mother . . ."

"Our own boat?" David asked, his voice excited for the first time since he had walked down the steps from the plane.

"Yeah. If I bought it, we could take passengers with us on cruises around the Caribbean. That's the way we'd pay for it. But we'd only take people who enjoy sailing, stay out as long as we want to. You'd have your own cabin."

"That's super, Dad! When can we go?"

"Well, it'll take a while. First I'll have to put together enough money for a down payment."

"Sure," David said.

He'd heard enough promises during his ten years, Bradford realized. He turned to watch some kids playing at one of the booths, no longer looking into his father's face.

Bradford reached over and touched him on the shoulder.

"It's not going to be easy, David, but we're going to get that boat."

David turned to look at him again.

"Super," he said. But again there was an edge of hesitation in his voice.

Bradford looked at his watch.

It had taken more than an hour, but watches had been set up over all the vulnerable points. Ziggy had carried the Century Wheel to a place off the floor where he had begun work on a new panel to replace the one that was warped. Four security men were working overtime to carry out the spot checks on every fiftieth coin roll, and others had been instructed to increase their surveillance of every table, game, and slot in the Diamond Mine.

He knew there were undoubtedly other details he had overlooked, but he couldn't leave David waiting any longer at Circus-Circus. He was probably already sensing the crisis around him, feeling that Bradford was really too busy to spend the weekend with him.

But not this time: David wouldn't return to San Francisco feeling that his visit had been a nuisance, wondering why he had drawn those stars in the spaces on the kitchen calendar.

During the drive to Lake Tahoe, David laughed too quickly at Bradford's jokes, thanked him too many times for a couple of small presents, listened too intently when Bradford offered him advice about school. He also seemed to be watching for any sign of boredom in his father's face, ready to suggest that they cut the trip short.

Once they reached the lake he seemed thoughtful but relaxed. Louise had loved Tahoe and Bradford remembered the three of them walking along the shore, seeing the snow-covered mountain peaks reflected in the clear blue water, or taking out a bor-

rowed boat for a Sunday afternoon, far from the Diamond Mine and the gaudy world of Reno.

"I believe the cruise ship is going out soon, David.
Would you like that?"

"Do we have time, Dad?"

"We have time."

Once they were aboard, David began talking easily and naturally to Bradford and several of the other
passengers. The hesitation disappeared. For the first
time since Louise had taken David to San Francisco,
Bradford saw his son as he must appear to other
people—curious, eager, energetic, with sudden warm
flashes of humor. This was what he was missing—the
chance to see David being himself.

They looked down over the trees and the lake from one
of the roof-garden restaurants as they ate dinner.
Snow began to fall, lightly at first, then more heavily,
and by the time they reached the car for the drive back
to Reno the temperature had dropped to nineteen degrees.

There were some treacherous stretches between
South Lake Tahoe and Reno, and the roads could
glaze over quickly. Bradford concentrated on his driving and David said nothing until the most dangerous
part of the roadway was behind them.

Then he asked quietly, "If we did go down there,
where would we live? Could we stay on the boat all the
time?"

Bradford hesitated, feeling guilty now about mentioning the possibility.

"We'd spend a lot of time on it," he said after a few seconds, "but I think we'd have to have a house somewhere too—maybe in Nassau. I'll check on the schools there, find out how good they are. With the boat to move around on, we wouldn't have to be tied down to any one place. We could choose one of the other islands if we wanted to, or maybe live in Bermuda."

"Will it take long, you think? To get enough money to buy the boat?"

"It'll take a while. It depends on a lot of things."

"Does mother know? About the boat?"

"Not yet. I thought it would be better to wait until I have things pretty well worked out."

"Yeah. That would be better."

With David settled down in front of the television, Bradford glanced at his watch again.

"Will you be late for work, Dad?"

"A little."

"We could have come back earlier."

"I didn't want to come back earlier, David. This is one of the best days I've had in a long time."

"For me too, Dad. It was super."

Bradford saw the note as he turned on the lights in his office. It had been placed in a cleared space on the top of his desk:

Brad—

Will you come up to
my office as soon as you
arrive?

I'll be waiting, what-
ever the time.

Ned Crossley

He put the note in his pocket and headed for the
escalator.

◇

Diamond's office was dark. At nine-thirty on a Saturday night, that seemed strange. Bradford walked past
it down the hall toward Crossley's office.

As he passed through the anteroom usually occupied by Crossley's secretary, Bradford saw Crossley
hunched over his desk, his attention focused on some
sheets of paper neatly lined up before him. Under the
stark light of the desk lamp his face looked bloodless,
the carefully combed gray hair as lifeless as paper.

Bradford wondered again, as he had often over
the last fifteen years, what was concealed behind that
mask. Crossley had once been a boy, an adolescent, an
ambitious young man leaving home to make his fortune. But it was impossible now to see any trace of
those earlier existences in that cold, expressionless
face. It was as though he had been born in this office,
under that glaring light, with those pages spread out
there before him.

Yet his presence at the Diamond Mine was accidental, like the presence of most of the people who worked here. Chuck Grogan, who knew something about the personal lives of everyone around them, said that Crossley had been on his way to San Francisco and the promise of a job there when the train he was riding derailed just outside Reno. During the twenty-four hour delay while he and the other passengers were waiting for another train, he met Charlie Diamond, and by the time it took for them to have a cup of coffee together he had accepted a temporary job with Diamond.

Diamond had just opened the Diamond Mine the week before. It was in a little one-story building, long since torn down, and it had three card tables and a dozen creaky, outdated slot machines.

As the casino grew, someone had to be in charge of all the figures and Diamond had gradually turned that responsibility over to Crossley.

It was like gauging flowing water, keeping the shift-by-shift records of money passing through the Diamond Mine. Cash did not remain carefully counted and bundled and put away in drawers as it did in a bank. The same hundred-dollar bill which one player lost at a 21 table might have to be paid out a short time later to a winning poker player, and without the detailed work by someone like Crossley there would be no record of the player's loss at the 21 table or the player's win at poker. Hundreds of people were each handling many thousands of dollars in cash and chips twenty-four hours a day. Change boys and change girls, who were among the most miserably paid of all casino workers, would walk around with several hundred dollars each in their change aprons.

During the busiest hours a million dollars or more would move swiftly back and forth across the tables, to and from the counting room and the coin room, always at risk—not so much to lucky players as to dishonest employees and cross-roaders. The money moved restlessly hour after hour and when it disappeared it left little visible trace.

Someone had to retrace this intricate flow, to be able to say exactly how much money was in play during any shift, to calculate what percentage the casino was holding from every dollar bet at every table and every slot, to sound a warning signal when any of the casino games failed to produce the predicted profit.

In most casinos men like Crossley were given points—a fraction of the owner's profit. The owners saw this as a way of making sure that their key men felt a strong self-interest in keeping the operation honest and profitable.

But that had never happened at the Diamond Mine. During the early years there wasn't much profit to distribute, and once the casino began to make money Diamond used most of it to finance expansion. By the time the Diamond Mine began to make even more money than was needed to build it up, the pattern had been set. Crossley's salary had increased steadily, but it was still a salary. Bradford wondered whether that seemed unjust to Crossley, who saw to it that Diamond's millions were safely locked away or invested.

Crossley raised his head slowly.

"Well, finally." he said.

"I just found your note," Bradford said.

"I left it on your desk two hours ago."

"My son's here from San Francisco, and I took him out to the lake. I would have been back earlier, but the roads are beginning to ice over and . . ."

Crossley leaned back in his chair.

"I haven't been away from this office except to sleep for the past five weeks. When the whole security system breaks down . . ."

"It hasn't broken down. I know we have some problems."

Crossley refused to accept the interruption.

". . . some people decide that they can get away with anything," he continued. "That's not hard to understand. When they see how long it is taking us to clear up one problem, even when we know which table is involved and which shift . . ."

"Kenneth told me that the hold was back to normal at table seven the first night after I returned from vacation."

"Of course it went back to normal," Crossley said impatiently. "They saw Charlie going up to the cat-walk for the first time in seven or eight years and they had the common sense to ease off at that table for a few days. But then they looked around for other weak spots. I don't know if they gaffed the Century Wheel or just discovered that it was warped, but it didn't take them long to turn it into a loser. And now they're draining away three or four thousand a day from the coin room."

"I have my security men checking every fiftieth roll of coins."

"I know about that," Crossley said. "Everybody in the place knows about it. You might as well have them opening the packs out on the sidewalk. But even that hasn't stopped them."

Crossley opened the center drawer of his desk and brought out some coin wrappers and some coins. He put them in three piles on the top of the desk.

"This roll of nickels was two nickels short. A dime was missing from this roll, and a quarter from this one."

"When did you pick those up?"

"I sent Kenneth down about two hours ago and asked him to buy rolls from every change boy and change girl he could see. He bought fifteen rolls and three of them were short. That's when I first went down to see if you were in your office."

"The three packs could have been packaged before we started our close surveillance."

"Then why is the hold from the slots down at least fifteen hundred dollars a shift?"

Bradford felt the pain sharpen in the back of his neck. "I don't know," he said.

Crossley brought his desk calendar closer and leaned over to read a note he had made on it. "You know a man named Phillips, Roland Phillips?"

"I don't think so."

"He's a security officer. He's at MGM now but he doesn't like it much—too big, too bureaucratic, he says. He prefers working in midtown, too. I've asked him to come by to see you next Tuesday morning at ten. He couldn't make it Monday."

"To see me?"

"I'd like you to talk to him, see what you think of him."

"All right. I can always use another man."

Crossley frowned.

"I wasn't thinking of him as just another man. He could work along with you, taking over a few of your responsibilities."

"I'm not sure I understand what you mean."

"I thought he could oversee the coin room and the catwalk while you concentrate on the main floor, watching over the tables and the slots."

"That's what I used to do when Eddie Wolfe was here."

"It's just an idea. We can work out the details later."

"I'd like to discuss this with Charlie."

"Not now, Brad. He woke up this morning with a fever of a hundred and three, and his doctor gave him strict orders to stay in bed until it gets down to normal."

"I want to talk to him before I see Phillips."

"We'll see. We'll see."

Crossley rubbed a hand across his forehead.

"We are going to have to have some people we can trust watching over the coin room twenty-four hours a day. I've spoken to Tim."

"O'Rourke? I need him on the catwalk."

"Once this is cleared up he can go back on the catwalk. It's far more urgent to stop the skimming than to catch a couple of penny-ante cross-roaders."

"I don't know how Tim will take that."

"He's in the coin room now. I would have checked with you before moving him, but since you were late . . ."

"Then who's on the catwalk?"

"That's what I've been waiting to work out with you. I thought Chuck Grogan could go up there for a few nights, maybe a week."

"Chuck has never worked on the catwalk."

"That may be an advantage."

"He won't like it. Chuck enjoys being in the middle of things."

"I hope Chuck will be reasonable. If I'd had my way, he'd have been fired three years ago when he first began showing up half drunk. When you talk to him, it might be good to tell him that we're counting on him, that this is a chance for him to prove that Charlie was right in keeping him on."

Listening to Crossley, Bradford remembered what Chuck had once said about him. "The temperature drops seven degrees when he enters a room."

It wasn't going to be easy, Bradford realized as he sat having coffee with Chuck in the Golden Bowl, the lunch room which still served forty-nine cent breakfasts and dollar-nineteen steak dinners long after many of the casinos had discarded the tradition of serving meals at a loss. Diamond was convinced that players who came for the cheap food then paused at the slots on the way out and ended up spending more than they would have at a luxury restaurant.

Chuck began reminiscing. He had a selective memory about what he'd seen in his years as a dealer and a pit boss. He could forget the thousands who had been bankrupted by their gambling while he watched, and he remembered with a kind of boozy sentiment all the rare acts of benevolence by casino operators—especially Pappy Smith of Harolds Club.

"It must've been in '43 or '44," Chuck said. "I saw a young lieutenant come in, eyes all glassy, face white as a sheet. He asked me where he could find Pappy, and I went back to Pappy's office with him.

"The lieutenant was in charge of the PX over at Stead, and I heard him tell Pappy that he'd gambled away $2500 of the PX money. He'd lost it all over the weekend, he said, and nobody had discovered it was missing yet. But they were bound to find out the next morning when the commanding officer would be coming by to inspect the books. The lieutenant was certain that he'd be court-martialed, and he'd end up spending three or four years in the brig.

" 'This $2500,' Pappy said, 'did you lose it all at Harolds Club?'

"The lieutenant was perfectly honest about it. 'God, no,' he said. 'I must've been to every place in town where you can bet a nickel. I'd lose in one casino and I'd go to the next. I'd lose more there and by the time the night was over I probably went into fifteen places, losing in every damned one of them.'

"Pappy always carried a big roll of bills with him. I remember him reaching into his back pocket and taking out that roll, wrapped in a rubber band, and peeling off hundred-dollar bills.

" 'Okay, Lieutenant,' he said, putting twenty-five hundred dollar bills in his hands. 'I just ask you to promise me one thing. Promise me that you'll never gamble again as long as you live.'

"Usually when Pappy gave a loser enough cash for him to pay his motel bill or buy a bus ticket he'd say, 'I hope this will teach you not to gamble. But nobody's perfect, and if you decide you *have* to gamble again, promise me you'll do it at Harolds Club.' He didn't say it that time. He did a lot of joking with the players usually, but whenever I saw him later that evening he looked kind of sad, thinking about what could have happened to that young lieutenant."

Before Grogan could begin another story, Bradford cut in. "Chuck, I need your help," he said.

Grogan looked surprised.

"It's just for a few nights. I need someone I can trust up on the catwalk."

"Is Tim sick?"

"No, he'll be working for a few days in the coin room."

"You know I'd like to help, Brad, but I've never worked on the catwalk."

"I know. But you know how cross-roaders operate, what to watch for."

"There must be somebody who could do it better than I could."

"Ned asked me to ask you."

"Crossley? I thought he hated my guts."

"Ned doesn't like anybody. But he trusts you."

"Just for a few days, you say?"

"That's right. As soon as I can work things out, you'll be back down on the floor here."

"Well, if you think it will help."

As they started out of the Golden Bowl, Grogan touched Bradford's arm.

"Did Larry reach you?" he asked.

"Larry? No."

"He was going to try to call you at your apartment today. He has something on his mind."

"Did he say what?"

"No, but he must've heard about all the concentration on table seven. Everybody in the place knows."

"I'd like to talk to him. When's his next break?"

"He's not in yet."

"Not in? Has he changed shifts?"

"No, but his girl is being tested for a television commercial by some outfit in San Francisco, and he asked me if it was okay if he drove her over. I told him okay as long as he was back here by nine-thirty, when the heavy action starts."

Bradford looked at his watch.

"It's ten-thirty now," he said.

"I heard there was snow in the mountains. That could've slowed him down."

"Maybe that's it," Bradford said. "Would you let me know as soon as he comes in? I'd like to talk to him, find out what's bothering him."

"Fine, Brad. I'll tell him."

◇

The call from Lt. Tremont in the traffic department came at eleven-forty-five that night.

"You have an employee over there named Stevenson? Larry Stevenson?"

"Yes, we do."

"I'd like to get the names of his next-of-kin."

"Why?" Bradford asked, knowing the answer before he heard it.

"There's been an accident."

The car had tumbled nearly two thousand feet down the mountainside, turning over and over as it fell, crashing into sharp outcroppings along the way.

"It was like driving over a block of ice," a highway officer told Bradford. "And he must have been going seventy or eighty miles an hour."

"Larry would know better than to speed along this stretch," Bradford said.

"Most people know better, but once they get a few drinks in them . . ."

"I've never seen him drunk," Bradford said.

"Maybe he lost control, then. You can see where the car demolished the guard rails along there."

"What are the chances of finding out what caused the wreck?"

"I doubt if we'll ever know for sure. It took 'em nearly an hour to get the body out. Had to cut through the metal with blow torches."

"I'd like to know whether there was anything wrong with the brakes. If someone tampered with them."

The officer looked doubtful.

"We'll see what we can do," he said. "It's a helluva place to work down there. And we'll have to wait for the weather to clear a little before we can bring the car up."

◇

Poor Larry. Caught in the middle.

Bradford looked down at him now, and thought of the fantasies that had made up his life. Yale graduate, he had told some, although he had never been near Yale. Boxing champion, heir to a shipping fortune, nephew of an enormously wealthy Brazilian rancher. . . .

At least all the illusions had not died before Larry did. Even here in this grim morgue there was something eternally hopeful in that young face.

The tales of imaginary wealth would not have fooled Melanie. The preacher's boy from Kansas, caught up in a passionate affair with an astonishingly beautiful girl for the first time in his life, had been ready to risk everything to keep her. That explained the hurried trip to Chicago, a session with the salesman with a false booming laugh, the amateurish scam with the expensive cylinder.

But somewhere along the way the attempt to skim away enough money to give Melanie her chance in television had collided directly with the schemes of someone far more ambitious—and far more knowledgable about casinos—than Larry.

Someone far more ambitious, far more devious. Someone who knew far more about how the Diamond Mine worked.

· 8 ·

The Hidden Pattern

"I guess I better get out to the gate, Dad," David said.

"There's no rush, David. I don't think they'll call your flight for another twenty minutes."

"I like to watch the planes coming in."

"All right. I'll go along with you."

"That's okay, Dad. I know you're busy."

"Well, if you're sure you'll be all right."

"Yeah, I'll be fine."

"I'll call later today to make sure you got home all right."

"Fine, Dad. If you have time."

David paused at the end of the first section of the passageway and looked back. Bradford waved, and he saw David give a tentative wave with his free hand before heading on.

◇

"I tried to let him make his own decisions," the Reverend John Stevenson said as Bradford drove him to the morgue. "It worried his mother, his working at a casino, but I thought it was best if we didn't interfere. I just hoped he wouldn't stay too long."

He spoke very quietly. He looked like an older and more serious Larry—a few pounds heavier, the hair a little thinner, the easy smile long vanished. A Larry who had been disappointed often enough so that he no longer expected much from the world and had no vivid illusions to sustain him.

This was no dark figure thundering from the pulpit during Larry's childhood, Bradford realized. A sad, thoughtful, puzzled man. Twice on the ride in from the airport he had spoken of Larry as though he were still living: "Larry likes . . ." and "Larry believes . . ."

When they reached the morgue Bradford offered to go in with him.

"Thank you, Mr. Bradford. That won't be necessary."

As he reached for his flight bag, he asked, "Do you have a son?"

"Yes, a boy of ten."

"I hope all goes well with him."

He stepped out of the car and Bradford watched him enter the morgue to make arrangements to take his son home to Kansas.

◇

There it was, on the top of the desk. A Xerox copy of the signed note: Eighteen thousand dollars borrowed from the Reno National Bank, interest at the rate of 12½ percent, first monthly payment of four hundred and fifty dollars due in just over two weeks.

He should have assumed that the note could not remain a secret. Nothing did in Reno. The entire city was watched over twenty-four hours a day. It was as though there were a thousand unsleeping observers up there above them all, walking endlessly along some enormous interweaving catwalk.

It was strange. For fifteen years he had felt that he was one of the watchers. Now suddenly he knew he was one of those being watched.

It made him realize far more sharply than ever before how vulnerable the dealers and the pit bosses and the floormen must feel, why they listened for the soft footsteps above them, how conscious they were of the unseen eyes.

He studied the copy closely. The typed letters were sharp and clear. It had been made from the original kept by the bank, not from the carbon copy which Tompkins had given him to take with him.

Obtained by someone who could get anything he wanted from the Reno National Bank because he was one of their most important customers. Someone whose requests could not be refused.

Crossley?

◇

At three-thirty in the morning, exhausted but not able to sleep, Bradford turned that possibility over and over in his mind.

At first it all seemed to fit together.

After Larry's trip to Chicago and his return with the cylinder, he had probably used it cautiously at first. But Crossley, analyzing the reports from each table for each shift with the extraordinary sensitivity to figures he had developed over the past forty years, probably became aware the morning after the cylinder was first put into use.

Was it something he had been watching for, waiting for? A genuine scam which involved a moderate amount of money, a trifling loss to the Diamond Mine, but which could be used to camouflage a far more ambitious and devious plan of his own?

As the keeper of all the records, Crossley had unlimited opportunities to juggle the figures from every activity in the casino, hour by hour, shift by shift, day by day. He could make a minor scam carried on by an amateur like Larry appear to be a major threat to the casino.

But he must have realized that exaggerating the loss from a single 21 table would not be enough by itself to explain a raid of the size he wished to make on the Diamond Mine. When he examined the shift figures closely and realized that the Century Wheel was behaving erratically, actually allowing a few of the players who happened to place their money on the twenty to walk away with a win of two or three hundred dollars, he had probably listed losses four or five times that large on his sheets summarizing each day's results. Then, when a couple of customers complained of being shortchanged—a dangerous complaint, but one that had been made before in the Diamond Mine and other casinos without causing a crisis—he had succeeded in focusing Diamond's suspicions on the poor middle-aged women who had worked at their monotonous jobs for decades.

Crossley must have recognized that the sequence of crises would arouse the interest and curiosity of Tim O'Rourke, Chuck Grogan, and Bradford. They would be in positions to discover that the trouble at table seven, the problems with the Century Wheel and the supposed skimming by the women in the coin room had all been either invented or grossly exaggerated. Because he knew the three of them were very familiar with all the operations of the Diamond Mine and were most likely to suspect the figures given in the daily summaries and those listed in the Monday reports, he had set out to raise questions about their competence. When he failed to convince Diamond that Chuck Grogan should be fired because of his drinking and that Tim O'Rourke was now too old to work on the catwalk during the busiest hours of the evening, he had shifted them to jobs in which they would be less competent, away from their long familiar territory. If he had merely felt that someone should be assigned to watch over the coin room for a week or two, why hadn't he asked Grogan to move there? Obviously because that would leave O'Rourke up on the catwalk— unblinking, eternally alert, incorruptible—roaming endlessly over the wooden planks, moving sinuously past all obstacles, watching for any false moves on the main floor. When another week or two went by without any real sign that cross-roaders were draining thousands of dollars a day from the Diamond Mine, O'Rourke would begin asking questions. Dangerous questions for Crossley.

The next step would be the hiring of Phillips— a security man Bradford had never heard of, although the world of security men in Reno was fairly small and he was familiar with most of them. Crossley had chosen his words very carefully. "To work with you," he had said. Not "work for you."

Once supervision of the catwalk and the coin room and probably later the counting room was in the hands of his new security man, not yet familiar enough with the Diamond Mine to guard it efficiently, indebted to Crossley for his appointment, the casino would be open to systematic, unlimited looting. It could go on for months before it was detected, as it had in some Vegas casinos.

Bradford reached for a scrap of paper and began making notes about the puzzling events of the past five weeks—while he was away and since his return:

Marked cards taken from my office by someone. Who?
   Why?
Trouble at table seven. How much taken by Larry?
   How much reported taken on Monday reports?
The problem with the Century Wheel. Was it just
   warped? Or gaffed? Were the figures about the
   decrease in the hold real or exaggerated? (No one
   seemed to be betting on the twenty while we were
   watching. If the wheel had been gaffed, wouldn't
   someone be there, betting heavily?)
Had the weighted stone found in the wastebasket near
   the Century Wheel been used? Or was it put there
   just to confuse us, make us believe the wheel had
   been gaffed?
The coin rolls. Why only six of them found short with
   all our checking? And all six found by Ken
   Warner—three while I was in Chicago, three Saturday night when I was on my way back from
   Tahoe.
Copy of the loan agreement left on my desk. Who left
   it? Why?

   Suddenly as he looked back over the list, he realized that on at least three of the occasions he had listed
Kenneth Warner was involved. He was the one who
found the weighted stone. He was the one who first reported that customers were complaining about being
shortchanged, and he was the one who went down to
the main floor on Saturday night to carry out a spot
check for Crossley and had returned with three rolls he
said were short. No one else had turned up a single

short roll—none of the security men, none of the cashiers who had joined in the surveillance since Warner's first report.

Was it possible that Crossley and Warner had worked together, were still working together?

He considered that for a moment, then decided no.

Crossley trusted Ken more than he did most people, but Bradford had never seen any special warmth on either side. And both would recognize how dangerous it was to collaborate with anyone on a scam.

No, they wouldn't have worked together. It was one or the other.

Crossley alone?

It was difficult to come up with any convincing reason why he would set out to destroy a business he'd devoted his life to building.

There might be some jealousy, of course. There was reason enough all around the Diamond Mine: Charlie Diamond's name emblazoned everywhere—on every slot machine, woven into the carpet, on every napkin used in the Golden Bowl, on five hundred billboards scattered across the west, glittering there in the Reno sky.

But that had been true from the beginning. Crossley must have realized early that Diamond would never share the center stage. Few of the old-time casino owners did. They had vassals, not partners.

Worry about the future? A sudden urgency to build up a stake to carry him through the years of his retirement?

That sounded more likely. All of the casinos were notorious for the stinginess of their provisions for employees who retired. Many of them offered no pension plans at all, and the one belatedly introduced at the Diamond Mine was completely inadequate.

But Crossley had been paid well for forty years and he had always lived abstemiously. There were no children for him to leave money to.

No.

Not Crossley.

Ken Warner, acting alone, using his influence on Crossley, quietly building up the sense of crisis.

Bradford was almost certain now. If one more piece fell into place. . . .

He looked up the telephone numbers of the security man, Roland Phillips, and Caleb Tompkins of Reno National Bank.

He made notes of the numbers, then looked at his watch. He couldn't possibly call Phillips and Tompkins at three-forty-seven a.m. They would be too irritated to answer his questions, to give him the information he needed.

He settled back on the pillow. He should wait until at least six-forty-five but he couldn't do that. He'd let them have another hour and a half of uninterrupted sleep, then . . .

He was certain in his own mind now, but he felt the need for just one or two more pieces of the puzzle before he talked to Diamond.

Warner must have realized soon after he went to work for Crossley that he was in a pivotal position. All the raw figures came to him—from the coin room, from the cashiers, from the counting room. And he was the one who recorded the drop (the amount played) and the hold (the amount kept by the Diamond Mine) on every game, shift by shift, day by day, week by week. He was the one who compared the results with those of the same shift a year earlier, two years earlier, five years earlier. And he was the one who supervised the daily transportation of cash to the Reno National Bank—the last one to check the contents of the huge metal boxes crammed full of hundred-dollar bills and five-hundred-dollar bills sent over for storage in the vaults reserved for the Diamond Mine and those reserved for the personal wealth of Charlie Diamond. Warner prepared the daily records of deposit, then took them in to Ned Crossley for his signature.

The temptation must have been enormous from the beginning. All that concentrated power—something Diamond had guarded against everywhere else in the casino—must have mesmerized Ken. Probably in the early months he just dreamed about what it would be like, skimming off a few hundred dollars a day from the hundreds of thousands he was overseeing. When he did finally decide to try it, he had begun modestly. According to the Monday reports, Warner had probably taken only a few hundred dollars the first week Bradford was in the Bahamas. But he'd doubled the amount the next week, increased it again the third week, and now if Crossley's estimates were right he was taking two or three thousand a day. Like all gamblers, he could not stop with a small win.

◇

At five-forty, Bradford dialed Roland Phillips' number.

"Mr. Phillips?"

"Yes." Phillips had obviously been asleep. "Who is this?"

"Don Bradford. I'm the chief security officer at the Diamond Mine."

"Oh, yes."

"I'm sorry to call so early, but I won't be near a phone for a while and I wanted to confirm the time for our appointment Tuesday morning."

"I see."

Phillips sounded guarded. A little doubtful.

"Is ten still all right with you?"

"Oh, yes, that'll be fine. If it's convenient for you."

"Yeah. Well, fine." Bradford paused. "We haven't said anything outside about needing a new security officer. I was just wondering how you happened to hear about the possibility of a job with us. Are you a friend of Ned's?"

"Mr. Crossley? No, actually I've never met him."

"But you do know someone who works for us?"

"Well, I went to school . . ."

Phillips hesitated.

". . . someone I went to school with just happened to mention that there might be an opening over there."

"Who was that, Mr. Phillips?"

"Oh, I don't think you'd know him. Man named
. . ." He hesitated again. ". . . Adderly."

"No, that name doesn't sound familiar."

"Well, then, I'll see you at ten Tuesday morning," Phillips said, eager to close off their conversation.

"Fine. See you then."

There was another pause, then a click on the
other end of the line.

The call hadn't told him as much as he'd hoped.
But Phillips had behaved exactly as he would have if
he were a friend of Ken Warner's, under instructions
not to use Warner's name when he came in for the interview. And it seemed certain now that he was not a
friend of Crossley's. Someone must have directed him
to Crossley, since ordinarily an applicant for a job in
security would begin by talking to the casino's chief security officer.

"Who is this?" Caleb Tompkins asked at the third ring
of the telephone.

"Don Bradford."

"What time is it?"

"I'm afraid it's very early, but I need to check on
one thing with you."

"If it has something to do with the bank . . ."

"It's about my loan agreement," Bradford said.
"Someone left a copy of it on my desk."

"Oh."

There was a long pause, then Tompkins said, "I'm sorry about that, Mr. Bradford. I said that we had no right to release a copy of the agreement without your permission. But the president said we had no choice, since the request came from Mr. Crossley's office."

"From Ned?"

"Not directly from Ned. From that young assistant of his."

"You sent it to Ken Warner?"

"Actually, we didn't send it. He came over to the president's office to pick it up. For Ned, he said."

"So you haven't actually talked to Ned about it?"

"No. Just young Warner."

Diamond was still groggy from the sleeping pill the doctor had insisted on his taking, and at first Bradford wasn't sure how many of the details he was absorbing. But after Bradford had covered most of his list, Diamond asked, "No one else has found any coin rolls short but Kenneth?"

"That's right."

"And he was the one who first told Ned that something might be wrong at table seven?"

"That's what Ned told me. I talked to him just before I came up to see you."

"And Kenneth also raised the first question about the Century Wheel?"

"Yes. Ned says he came over looking puzzled and

asked him if it was possible for the Century Wheel to lose money."

"And this security officer—what's his name?"

"Phillips."

"Kenneth was the one who suggested that he talk to Ned about a job without saying that he was an old school friend of Kenneth's?"

"That's my guess."

"He thought of almost everything, didn't he?"

"Just about."

Bradford hesitated a few seconds, but he realized he had no choice. "There's one other thing. I owe Reno National Bank eighteen thousand dollars, and when I came back last night from picking up Larry's father I found a copy of the loan agreement on top of my desk."

Diamond reached over and picked up a folded paper from the small chest of drawers next to his bed.

"A copy like this one?" he asked.

Bradford unfolded the paper. Another copy of the loan agreement.

"Yes," he said. "Exactly like this one."

"Somebody must have shoved that under my door during the night. The maid found it on the floor when she brought me a cup of coffee a few minutes ago."

"I guess I should have mentioned the loan to you," Bradford said.

Diamond waved the thought away with his hand.

"Nothing wrong with a bank loan," he said. "I

wouldn't want you borrowing money on the street."

"I never have."

"I know."

Diamond reached for the telephone and dialed Kenneth Warner's number.

"Is that you, Kenneth?"

A brief pause.

"Better now. I had a fairly restful night."

Another pause.

"Would you come up, Kenneth? I'd like to see you about something."

He put down the phone.

"Shall I stay? Bradford asked.

"No, I don't think that will be necessary," Diamond said. "Something like this, I prefer to handle myself."

"Okay."

"But you might leave me those notes you made. Just as a reminder."

An hour later, Bradford saw Kenneth Warner heading for the street. His face was drawn and pale, and he did not pause to look back.

· 9 ·

Diamond's Toke

Just after nine Monday evening Bradford's phone rang.

"Brad, do you have a minute?"

The deep voice again. It sounded a little hoarse but not as tired as it had since Bradford's return from the Bahamas.

"Yes, I do."

"Would you drop by?"

"I'll be right up."

◇

Diamond was waiting near the door. He motioned Bradford into his office, then walked over to his desk and opened the center drawer.

"I stopped by Harrah's a few minutes ago," he said. "Picked up a few chips."

So this is my toke, Bradford thought. I've saved the Diamond Mine from Ken Warner and a scam that could have cost two or three hundred thousand dollars, maybe more, and he's about to toss me a few chips, like any winning gambler.

How much? he wondered. Five thousand? No—more than that. Diamond had given him five thousand as a Christmas bonus during one very profitable year three years before.

Diamond began taking hundred-dollar chips out of the drawer and arranging them in stacks, his long fingers moving with the skill traceable to the years in the late thirties and early forties when he occasionally took over a table when one of his dealers failed to appear.

Ten chips in each stack. Twenty-five stacks.

A twenty-five-thousand-dollar toke.

He'd undoubtedly bought the chips with cash, Bradford realized, as casually as most men would pick up a new shirt. Cash lifted out of the steady stream of hundred-dollar bills flowing through the casino, on the way from the floor to the counting room. This way, there would be no written record on the books of the Diamond Mine, no check for twenty-five thousand dollars signed by Charlie Diamond which might arouse the curiosity of the auditors for the gaming commission, nothing anybody could trace.

Not that there was anything illegal about a bonus: casinos paid them regularly to their most valuable employees. But by paying this one in chips Diamond would not have to explain to anyone why he had given a bonus of this size in the month of September. He would not have to mention Ken Warner's scam to anyone outside. A small problem involving a dishonest employee had been quietly resolved—no point in troubling anyone else with it.

Diamond had another reason for giving him his reward in chips, Bradford realized. To cash them in, he would have to cross the floor at Harrah's on his way to one of the cashier's counters. Diamond was counting on him pausing on the way at one of the 21 tables, just for a few hands. And once Bradford had made those first bets, Diamond knew what would happen next. If Bradford were winning there at the beginning, he would keep playing, raising his bets, certain that he was about to turn the twenty-five thousand into fifty or a hundred thousand. If he were losing at first, he would begin doubling, then redoubling his bets, certain that his luck would change.

That's what Diamond was expecting. After all, his fortune had been built on those twin delusions which doomed all gamblers: the winner's certainty that he would keep on winning, the loser's delusion that the cards couldn't possibly be against him, that he was bound to win if he kept playing long enough.

If Diamond hadn't felt sure that Bradford would

gamble the twenty-five thousand away, he wouldn't
have given him that large a toke. He knew the amount
was large enough to make it possible for Bradford to
leave the Diamond Mine, to leave Reno, to start over
somewhere else. He was an old man, shaken by the experience with Warner, and he would not feel comfortable with a new chief security officer.

Looking at the generous stacks of chips, Bradford
understood that. Diamond was betting on his weakness. He'd undoubtedly learned about that disastrous
evening at Paradise Island soon after it occurred. It
was a small world, the world of the casino owners, and
useful information did not take long to travel across it.
Someone observing from the floor or the catwalk that
evening had undoubtedly gotten word back to Diamond quickly, counting on some future favor in return.

Even though he recognized the motives behind
the toke, Bradford couldn't turn it down. That would
be an unforgiveable insult.

"Thank you very much," he said. "I didn't expect . . ."

Diamond cut in quickly. He was always uncomfortable with thanks.

"You'll need something to carry those in," he
said.

He looked around, found the shopping bag from
Harrah's which he'd probably used to bring them in,
then discarded it. Bradford saw that it offended his
sense of dignity to haul twenty-five thousand dollars so
unceremoniously. He reached for his new pigskin
briefcase.

"I can't take that," Bradford said, knowing that in some strange way the luxurious new case meant more to Diamond than the twenty-five stacks of chips.

Diamond was already emptying some papers from it.

"You can bring it back tomorrow," he said.

After you lose these at Harrah's.

There was no question: He looks at me and he sees a gambler. A gambler with more self-control than most, like an alcoholic who has demonstrated that he can occasionally go for months without taking a drink. But still a gambler. He sees it as clearly as I see that a man has a potbelly or a broken leg.

As Diamond held the briefcase opened and dropped the chips into it, Bradford heard the soft, dry cough again. He said nothing, pretending that he hadn't noticed.

But Diamond surprised him by commenting on it himself. "They don't know what causes it," he said. "They tell me it could be the drop in temperature at night here, and they want to send me off to some place in Arizona for two or three months to see if that makes any difference. You ever been to Arizona?"

"I've passed through a couple of times, but I've never really spent any time there."

"Wall-to-wall retirement villages, that's all it is. Old men sitting in the sun wearing Hawaiian shirts, waiting for their next heart attack. Gets cold there too when the sun goes down. I told my doctor that, but he just laughs. If a doctor can't cure you, he wants to get rid of you, get you out of his sight. While this one is telling me I should go to Arizona, another doctor in

Arizona is trying to pack all the patients he can't cure off to New Mexico or Nevada. Die out of sight, that's what they want us to do. Surrounded by fat wheezing old men in Hawaiian shirts."

He closed the briefcase and handed it to Bradford.

"Wait a second and I'll walk down with you," he said. He put the papers he'd taken from the briefcase in the center drawer and locked the desk.

Bradford paused just outside the door. A new bank of slot machines had been installed no more than five feet from Diamond's office. This had been empty space, and it had bothered Diamond every time he passed through it. Like most old-time casino owners in Reno, Diamond saw unoccupied space as lost income, and wherever he could see a way to jam in one or two new slots he did.

Diamond led the way through a cluster of old women in polyester pantsuits crowded around the new machines.

"One thing about this business," he said, "you can't relax, decide that everything is under control, nothing can go wrong. I've seen too many owners try that in the last thirty or thirty-five years, and things just fall to pieces around them. Take young Warner now—who'd have expected him to try anything like this? Twenty-five years old, excellent job, reasonable salary—much better than he'd get if he were working for a bank or an insurance company—good chance to move up when Ned retires in three or four years— why did he risk everything?"

They were passing through a crowd of middle-aged housewives risking the family grocery money, old men and old women taking a chance with their Social Security checks, probably here and there a frightened clerk or bookkeeper gambling with money he was supposed to be safeguarding. And yet Diamond could ask with genuine puzzlement why a twenty-five-year-old employee might be ready to take a risk which could offer him freedom from the prospect of working long hours in an office for forty more years. Work which had one principal purpose: to add to the obscene fortune Diamond's heirs—cousins and nephews he cared nothing at all about—would inherit when the old man finally died.

"If he felt I wasn't paying him enough, all he had to do was to come by to see me," Diamond said as they moved down the crowded escalator. "I don't believe in overpaying a boy who's still in his twenties, could get him into bad habits, actually hurt him over the years. But another forty or fifty a week, that I'd 've considered."

Diamond paused.

"One thing sure," he said. "He won't be back."

"And the money?" Bradford asked.

Diamond touched the jacket of his expensive gray suit, patting something he had in his pocket.

"I have his marker," he said.

His marker. His I.O.U.

What was it? Bradford wondered. A letter to Warner's bank asking them to turn the stolen funds over to Diamond? A cashier's check for the amount he had taken? Keys to his safe deposit box? Or a signed confession of his skimming, to be produced only if he reappeared in Reno? Whatever it was, it was enough to make Diamond feel that Warner would be of no future danger to the Diamond Mine. The anxiety of the past few weeks had disappeared and he seemed to feel a sense of triumph about the speed with which the potentially disastrous scam had been short-circuited.

As they crossed the main floor, Bradford started to ask where Warner was. On his way to Vegas? He might be. "Go take a swim with the piranhas if you want to," Diamond had told a pit boss who had been caught cheating shortly after Bradford came to work for him. Victimization of Vegas casino owners did not disturb him, except when the schemes that succeeded there reminded him of possible future threats to the Diamond Mine.

At the door, Diamond turned to face Bradford.

"About Larry," he said softly. "Is it possible that he really wasn't guilty?"

"I don't know," Bradford said. "There was that cylinder."

"But Ken Warner could have planted that in the girl's apartment, couldn't he? They could have even been working together, Warner and the girl, with Larry caught in the middle."

"Yes, that's possible," Bradford said.

It would be more comfortable for Diamond to believe that a young dealer he had liked and trusted had not betrayed him. And did it really matter a damn now whether Larry was innocent or not? The people who gambled and lost at table seven during those weeks would have lost just as much whether or not Larry was occasionally handing Melanie a cylinder loaded with hundred-dollar chips. And what difference did it really make to Diamond's future heirs that there might be a few thousand dollars less left in the stacks piled away in his vault at Reno National?

In any case, whether he had taken the money or not, poor Larry was beyond the reach of security now, no longer under surveillance from the catwalk.

As Bradford started out the door, Diamond touched his arm. "This has been a tough time for all of us. I don't think you've had more than four hours sleep any night since you came back from the Bahamas. Why don't you take a couple of days to rest up?"

And gamble away that twenty-five thousand.

Bradford hesitated a second, then said, "Thank you very much. If everything's settled . . ."

"Everything is under control," Diamond said.

"Louise?"

"Yes, Brad."

"How's David?"

"He's asleep."

"Oh."

Bradford glanced at his watch. Eleven-forty. It had taken a couple of hours to make sure that all the necessary arrangements were completed at the Diamond Mine, with Tim O'Rourke back on the catwalk and Chuck Grogan on the main floor.

"I was just thinking . . . I'd like to see him." And
then he added: "And you."

"What do you mean, Brad? He's just come back."

"Not here. I'd like to come there."

"When?"

"Tomorrow. If that would be possible."

She was waiting for him to say more, but it would
be better to do that when he was talking to her directly, not over the phone.

"There's no . . ." She hesitated. "No problem, is
there, Brad?"

"No, no. No problem at all."

"Well, then, fine. What time do you expect to get
here?"

"First flight I can get out tomorrow morning.
Could I call you from the airport as soon as I've picked
up my ticket?"

"All right."

He had to know one more thing.

"You haven't . . . seen anyone, have you?"

"You mean a lawyer?"

"Yes."

"No, I haven't, Brad."

"I'm glad. Maybe . . ."

"We'll see, Brad."

"Fine." And then he added: "Don't mention this
to David until I call tomorrow morning, okay? I'd like
to surprise him."

"No, I won't mention it."

There had been too many disappointments over
the eleven years since they were married, too many an-

nounced plans never carried out. She would wait until she was sure that he was actually at the airport, ticket in hand.

"I'll make my reservations now."

"Fine, Brad." And then she added, sounding more certain than she had in a long time: "See you tomorrow."

◇

He woke up, sweating in the cold Reno night. The fever was back—the fever he thought he had conquered. Again there was the temptation: the thought of the tables, the memory of the moments when anything seemed possible, the excitement of that instant when the cards were about to fall, still held there in the dealer's hand, the cards which could bring triumph or disaster.

He looked at the small travel clock on the chest of drawers next to his bed.

3:25.

Six long hours until his plane would be leaving, and he knew he wouldn't be able to get back to sleep.

He lifted himself on his elbows and looked out toward the scattered lights that always burned through the night, the faint distant moon, the stars in the dark blue sky.

Tomorrow he would be in a different world. It would never again be so simple to grab any clothes that happened to be handy, to walk down three flights of stairs, to step out into this universe which had been the center of his life for fifteen years.

It would be his farewell to Reno, his farewell to gambling.

He opened the briefcase which he'd placed under his pillow and counted out exactly twenty of the one-hundred-dollar chips. Two thousand dollars.

That was all. If he won, he could have an extra four thousand, maybe eight thousand, maybe ten thousand to help them start their new life in the Bahamas. If he lost . . .

He wouldn't lose.

He'd felt that that evening at Lake Tahoe when he had come out fifteen thousand dollars ahead. And he had felt it at Paradise Island, where he had actually doubled his money to thirty-six thousand dollars but then hadn't had the sense to quit.

Just one problem, he realized. To bet intelligently at 21, you should start out with forty times your basic bet. Not two thousand, but four thousand. He'd need forty of the one-hundred-dollar chips.

He wouldn't touch the rest. He would check the briefcase with a Harrah's cashier, where it would be as safe as though it had been placed under the protection of a Swiss banker. And before dawn he would cash in all the chips—the ones Diamond had given him and the ones he'd won.

There was a secret. He knew it, even if he'd sometimes ignored it. *Set a limit and don't change it.* Stop if you're losing, stop if you're winning.

If he doubled this four thousand, he would quit. If he lost this four thousand . . .

He wouldn't lose.

But if he lost this four thousand, he would quit.

He snapped the lock on the briefcase. Twenty-one thousand safely closed away in there: enough to start over in the Bahamas. The profits from the *Southern Wanderer* or some other boat like it would be enough for him to make the monthly payments on the boat and the four hundred and fifty a month to the Reno National.

He would choose a table with a two-hundred-dollar limit, but he would stay within his own self-imposed limit: one hundred dollars a hand.

And he wouldn't touch the money in the briefcase, no matter what happened. That money belonged now to Louise and David and the future.

◇

He pushed the first of the forty chips forward.

First card: a seven.

Second card: a ten.

Seventeen. Dangerously high to ask for a hit, but probably too low to win. The dealer had a face card showing.

Bradford nodded and the dealer flipped him another card.

A four.

Twenty-one.

◇

Sometimes he had a nineteen, sometimes a twenty, sometimes a twenty-one. When his cards were bad, the dealer went bust.

There were seventy-two of the hundred-dollar chips in front of him now. Players had drifted over from nearby tables to watch. Like catnip to a cat, the smell of a winner to the crowd in a casino. A gap-toothed man in a grimy workshirt kept pushing closer and closer, sharing in the suspense, keeping careful count of the number of unbroken wins, his eyes moving restlessly from the cards to the growing stack of hundred-dollar chips.

Eighty-three hundred dollars. Up from four thousand.

Bradford hesitated.

The gap-toothed man had offered no advice, but it was obvious what he was thinking.

You're betting too cautiously. With a run of luck like this, you should have five hundred dollars riding on every hand.

Five hundred would be too much, Bradford decided. But as far ahead as he was, he could double his bets to two hundred. After all, forty-three hundred of the eighty-three hundred there before him was really Bill Harrah's money. He would be betting on Harrah's chips.

He was about to double his bet when he looked up and saw "Lucky Dan," about twenty feet away. Going through his pockets desperately, searching for an overlooked dollar bill, fifty cents, a quarter, a dime. . . .

Bradford gathered up his chips.

"You're not quitting now, are you?" the gap-toothed man who had been standing at his elbow asked.

"Yep," Bradford said. "Now."

He flipped a hundred-dollar chip to the dealer, who was still young enough and inexperienced enough to be surprised.

"Thank you," the dealer said.

Bradford went over to the cashier's counter to pick up the briefcase, then cashed in all but two of the chips.

Twenty-nine-thousand dollars. He'd doubled the four thousand he'd gambled, and he'd quit. He had quit while he was winning.

On his way out, he paused near "Lucky Dan."

"I think you dropped these," he said, handing "Lucky Dan" two one-hundred-dollar chips.

"Lucky Dan" looked at him for a few seconds, studying his face, and Bradford wondered whether Dan was going to refuse them. But then the old man's thin fingers closed over the two chips.

He said nothing. He started for the same 21 table where Bradford had been playing, took the empty space Bradford had left open.

Bradford waited a few minutes at the door, watching.

"Lucky Dan" didn't change the one-hundred-dollar chips for smaller ones. As the game began, he put one of them down, then the second one. Although he didn't have another penny in the world, he was betting his last two hundred dollars on one turn of the cards.

Poor fool, Bradford thought. After losing all evening, he could at least have stretched this out, playing five-dollar chips or ten-dollar chips.

Then, as he watched, "Lucky Dan" reached out eagerly to draw in his winnings.

The two hundred had become four hundred.

Bradford felt a moment of extraordinary pleasure. It was totally illogical, he knew: "Lucky Dan" would now have the delusion that he was destined to win, that at last his luck had turned, that there were a whole series of triumphs there before him.

But now for this brief interlude at least the poor schmuck was not a loser.

Not wanting to see what happened next, Bradford strolled on out into the crowded street.

As the plane rose diagonally into the sky, Bradford took a last look down.

The valley looked beautiful and peaceful under the morning sun. The air was clean and clear, the landlocked seagulls were drifting lazily through the cloudless sky, the Truckee was flowing gently along the winding pathway it had traced over the centuries. And all around were the spectacular mountains, their sharp edges softened by the first snow of September.

Some time there in the distant future it would be good to come back to Reno for a weekend. As a tourist who knew that this was a place meant for a few hours, a brief escape from reality.

However long he waited, the town would still be there. It had tapped the one inexhaustible vein: Hope.

He watched as it disappeared into the distance.